Chapters

1. Reminiscing

2. Choices We Make

3. Burning Bridges

4. Spark The Match

5. Run Or Die

6. Family Ties

7. All Or Nothing

8. Man Overboard

9. Drastic Measures

10. Revenge Is the Best Dish

11. The Game Is Chess, Not Checkers

12. The Two Headed Snake

13. Caught In A Deadly Web

14. Friend Or Foe

STREET DREAMS
The Gift and the Curse

Chapter One
Reminiscing

For those who have had the pleasure of following my past and my story, you know of it all to this point. You know what I have endured over these years. This painful existence that I happen to call a life continues to be explosive. The more I dwell on it, the more I realize a man must know when he is up and when he is genuinely down. The hardest part for a career professional boxer or a prize fighter is knowing when he is down for good. I won't lie to anyone. It was a hard pill for me to swallow. I had completely ended that chapter in my life, for good and for a great reason. I had new goals, new plans, and primarily for people depending on me to be here for them. I had to fully let go of my past life and all that I had lost. The life of walking into a six-bedroom house with wall-to-wall of money in every room. Money that reaches fifteen-foot ceilings. Money that we knew we could never spend in two lifetimes—the wild nights with countless number of fine women in my bed. I was traveling the world carefree on my private jet. I had few real friends and a handful of family left.

I was now focused on my family, and I wanted to raise my children the best way I knew how. I wanted to right some of the wrongs I've done and live. I had a significant hand in destroying so many lives. From putting a countless number of bodies into the ground or whether I put them there personally or put the order in to do so. I ordered men and women to be tortured for information or to send messages to my revivals that we were not to be fucked with. I took fathers, mothers, brothers, and sisters away from many families for money, respect, power, loyalty, honor, or turf. We, better yet, I was a cancer on society. All for love and those street dreams. I blame myself for being undeniably selfish. My lust for money and ambition for power were my weaknesses, not my strengths. This same selfish desire is the reason why it has taken the lives of people I loved the most and dearest to my heart. I'm talking about my parents. Later in life, my little brother and my two cousins were taken from me as well. Even a woman I was once so in love with. At some point, a man needs to see the light that money isn't everything if the ones you love aren't here to share the riches with him. My curse is even deeper. My cousin Dane's girlfriend was pregnant with his baby when he died. To add extra topping that made matters worse, my little brother Andrew's wife was also pregnant with his son. I was responsible for raising my brother and cousin's kids as my own. I owe them that and so much more.

I loved every moment of the experience of being a father. Mainly because their children were a representation of them. I was able to hold on to each of them that way. With this new life, no one in my circle had to live in fear. No one had to live a life looking over their shoulders at every turn. That was a curse I had to bear alone. That was almost impossible for me to believe for years, even though I preached it daily. I didn't want my family to worry that they may be in danger. So, it was sleepless nights and cold sweats for me alone.

For the first eight to ten years, I was a worried wreck. If a car was tagging behind us on a Sunday drive for too long, I felt in my gut that my wife and I were at our end. My heart would drop if

I saw a group of well-dressed Hispanic men walking toward my family and me at the mall or restaurant.

Without subconsciously knowing it, I would find my hand on my gun way too many times. I had armed bodyguards with me and my family 90 percent of the time. I had refused to let my guard down for years. I kept thinking the cartel would eventually catch up to us. After taking out three of Colombia's most ruthless drug cartel members, I knew the bounty would always be on our heads, as well as anyone who was involved in their murders. That risk was so high. Something like a king's ransom! So, my remaining family, friends, and I took refuge in Europe for the past twenty years.

Our lives were blessed, and I raised my cousin and bothers son as well as my twins
Jaxon, my son, and Jaylyn, my daughter. My wife Angelina kept me sane from the emptiness I intended to endure for many years. Since my family's death, I really wasn't the same mentally. Life was incredible for me because we were finally free of the fear of anything happening to me or any of my family members. My life with Angelina as my loyal, loving wife was unbreakable. Our bond and her beauty never aged after twenty uncertain years. Every time I looked at her, it was like looking at her for the first time.

Angelina and I didn't just buy a house once we got to Europe. We built a detailed home large enough for our family in the south of France in a small town just outside of Vince. It was a beautiful ranch home that the kids referred to as the compound. They called it the compound because of the 20-foot-tall cement walls surrounding the house for almost a mile. There were over 100 video surveillance cameras on the outside of the property and another 65 cameras within the home itself. I went from employing a 100-arm guard to watch over our home to 15 after 20 years. Most of them were ex-French police officers. Besides the excessive armed manpower, the compound was beautiful if you could ever get a view over our high walls. We had 30 purebred horses and 22 beautiful gardens. Our home had indoor and outdoor pools and a grape field as far as the eyes could see. We had to turn millions of our dirty money into legitimate legal income. One of our most profitable new businesses was a wine refinery. I owned a luxury boatyard that built million-dollar yachts. As well as a company that purchased and built small luxury hotels.

I loved all of my children as if they were my own and made sure they had everything they needed and wanted. However, I had certain rules that they needed to follow, such as doing well in school, helping out at the refinery, showing respect, being honest, and putting our family first. When I say spoiled, I mean they drove late-model Porsches, Lamborghini's, and Ferraris to school. The highest fashion was the norm for my kids. It wasn't anything out of the normal surroundings in this area because we were twenty minutes from Nice, and all their peers were well off financially. Adlana had her driver and bodyguards that followed her everywhere she went once she stepped outside of our home, and her cars, I ensured, were all bulletproof. I took no chances when it came to my family.
Some would say I had an occasion with security and the well-being of the people around me. Every year, I seemed to update our security system. I wanted to know which system was new and which was on the CIA or Interpol level of security. Ernesto and I remained very close friends or more like brothers. His kids and mine grew up together and considered themselves like cousins.

Well, they call Ernesto their uncle, and he loved hearing it. When I left the United States, I went with a quarter of my hundred and thirty-five million dollars. I left the rest in ten safety deposit boxes in seven states, hoping one day, my kids would be able to get that money. I only stepped foot in the United States to visit my family's grave site, and I never stayed more than three hours in the States. Any longer than that would be risking my and my family's lives. The Feds, the mob, and the Colombians were still looking for us, as far as I knew.

Ernesto and his brother joined me and my family in the South of France, taking refuge along with us. The Hernandez brothers left Miami with what little they had stashed within their estate, seventy-five million between the two of them, and a vow to never step foot back on the home soil of Colombia. The Hernandez brothers had over seven hundred million in a single bank in Colombia. The two of them were afraid because they knew the cartel would never release the bounty on their heads even twenty years later. What the brothers did against the cartel was a death sentence. They would never settle with such disrespect by only killing the two brothers responsible for these actions. Instead, the cartel would take great pride in completely wiping out everyone one the brother love or call friend and family. Ernesto sometimes had too much pride and refused to take a dime from me over the years. It is hard to change when you have a custom of living a certain lifestyle, and Ernesto had a big extended family. They made some poor business choices over the years, and the brothers were burning through their money at an outrageous rate. Ernesto had a son, Jesus, who was the same age as Jax and Jaylyn, twenty years old. I did my best to send his family money before he had to ask for it. I wanted to keep him away from ever returning to that life. The mind of a drug lord is one that needs power and demands respect and riches. I, on the other hand, refused to lose anyone else I loved and called family.

Ernesto built three homes in France and one in Geneva for his mother and sisters. His brother's home was in the city of Nice and was only a few minutes' drive from his big brother's home. The biggest of all three homes was in the town of Monaco, which was Ernesto's, of course. All the homes had four to six-car garages, three pools, seven to ten bathrooms, and eight to fifteen bedrooms. His entire family had over twenty cars, and Ernesto enjoyed having his suits made weekly. We would charter a private jet every year for the whole family's vacation. Over the years, seventy-five million dollars could only go so far before the Hernandez brothers had to make a choice.

Chapter Two
Choices We Make

I didn't know that Ernesto and Huel felt that twenty years had passed. They looked a lot older, put on a few extra pounds, and even spoke English a lot better. For weeks, the brothers discussed their chances of flying into Colombia and walking into a bank they own. Turn full ownership of all their funds to their two oldest kids. They acquired the bank 30 years ago, and the same bank manager has been running it all these years. It would simply be a secret between them and the manager. A school friend they entrusted their bank to and have known and trusted for more than 40 years. No one in Colombia would ever find out they were even there. The kids could fly into Colombia whenever they wanted to and withdraw any amount of money, they saw fit since no one in the Cartel was ever aware that the Hernandez brothers had ever had kids. Now, the brothers weren't fools when it came to business and making money. Huel opened a high-end jewelry business, and Ernesto opened Two high-end luxury car dealerships. Both businesses combined make them a lot of money, but the two of them were used to spending millions of dollars a week. Those habits were hard for the Hernandez brothers to kick.

Ernesto's son Jesus and Huel's daughter Ana went with their fathers to Colombia. Huel had none of his military connections anymore, so they had to walk a thin wire while they were in Colombia. They stayed at a very low-key hotel in the town of Barrio San Jose. Barrio was a twenty-to-thirty-minute drive from the city and ten minutes from a small airfield where the plane was. Just in case anything went wrong, they were ready for whatever. The plan was to head into the bank first thing in the morning as they opened and transferred the accounts into the kids' names and make a withdrawal of fifty million dollars, which would take anywhere from six to eight hours to withdraw the funds. Ernesto hired five cops to help transport funds from the bank to the airfield. The plan seemed full proof, but the smallest crack can make a foundation collapse. While the transaction was taking place, Jesus saw a young lady who worked at his father's bank and decided to talk to her and see if he could get to know her.

Jesus: Es un día increíble hoy (It's an amazing day today!)

Michelle: Sí. (Yes, it is.)

Jesus: Mi nombre es Jesús. Jesus Hernandez (My name is Jesus. Jesus Hernandez.)

Michelle: Bueno es un placer de conocer a usted Sr. Hernandez puedes abrir una cuenta hoy en día, es hacer un depósito o retiro. (Well, it's a pleasure to meet you, Mr. Hernandez. Are you opening an account today, making a deposit or withdrawal.)

Jesus: Mi familia y yo a hacer un retiro bastante grande hoy que será bastante mucho tomar todo el día (My family and I will be making a pretty big withdrawal today, which will pretty much take all day.)

Michelle: ¡Qué bueno! (That is nice!)

Jesus: Bueno ya me voy bastante mucho estar aquí todo el día. ¿Puedo tener el honor de llevarte a cenar. (Well seeing as I'll pretty much be here all day. Can I have the honor to take you to dinner.)

Michelle: Soy lo siento Sr. Hernandez, pero la política del Banco no es citas empleados o clientes. (I'm sorry Mr. Hernandez but the policy at the bank is no dating employees or customers.)

Jesus: También aborda la política causa de propietario citas estoy seguro de que tengo el poder de cambiar la política. (Well does the policy address dating owner cause I'm pretty sure I have the power to change the policy.)

Michelle: (laughing) muy lindos pero los dueños de este banco son hermanos y nadie ha visto ninguno de ellos en más de veinte años. Lo que significa también deben ser bien en su final de los años cuarenta. Así que por favor intente otra vez. (Very cute but the owners of this bank are brothers, and no one has seen either of them in over twenty years. Which also means they should be well in their late forties. So please try again.)

Jesus: (Smiling) Me alegra saber mis empleados conocen su historia en la facilidad pero debe pedir a su Gerente del Banco quien soy. Bye-bye, beautiful! (I'm glad to know my employees know their history on the facility, but you should ask your bank manager who I am. Bye-bye, beautiful!)

Jesus: Si cambia de opinión Michelle mal estar encima allí bebiendo mi cognac. (if do change your mind Michelle I'll be sitting right over there drinking my cognac)

Michelle paid no real attention to Jesus and the nonsense he was talking about. She was pretty much accustomed to men walking into the bank trying to swipe her off her feet with their elaborate stories, but nothing like the one she had just heard. After an hour or two, she noticed Jesus and his family were still sitting in the lobby area with their security and five police officers heavily armed. The bank manager was personally attending to their every need with coffee, lunch, and just about anything they needed. Still, this was nothing to make her jump to the conclusion that this guy and his family really owned the bank until one of the older gentlemen lit a cigar in the bank, and the manager allowed it. Mr. Ortiz was strongly against anyone smoking in the bank, much less in his presence.

This made Michelle raise an eyebrow, so she then decided to dig for some information on Jesus Hernandez. So, she googled him, and every picture that surfaced looked like nothing like him—then googled the owners of the Hernandez Bank of Colombia. She found a lot of pictures of the owners and their connection to cartels. Many of the photos she came across looked like the two older gentlemen this Jesus was companying. The Hernandez brothers did own the bank. The pictures she found online were of men in their early thirties. If she was to bet money on it that these two men in the bank lobby were the owners, she was sure to win. The bank manager then walked over to her desk and, very nervous and somewhat afraid, asked for her assistance. He wanted her in the bank's vault to help count the funds. She somehow knew better than to ask any questions if Mr. Ortiz, a highly respected man in the community, seemed so timid around these men. He hurried her and a few others into the vault. This even made her mouth drop because Mr. Ortiz never allowed anyone in the vault unless you had been with the bank since he started or had been a part of his team for fifteen years or so.

Once Michelle walked into the bank vault, there were six bank guards along with seven other bank tellers with money counters in front of them and counting mountains of money. Mr. Ortiz ordered two of the banks' security to close the bank to everyone else. This caused all the tellers to talk quietly about this situation to each other as they counted. Every single person was curious to know who these men were. Michelle didn't know what to make of the situation at all. All she knew was that this was the most exciting event this bank had seen in years. Since the bank has been open, it has never been robbed, unlike most of the large banks in the city. By the end of the day, Michelle witnessed the two Hernandez brothers go into a private vault. Once she saw that, there was no more question in her mind. The men were the Hernandez brothers. They had to be because the private vault was said to be where the cartel stored mountains of gold. She had stories saying the brothers who owned the bank were the only two people who had access to that vault.

As she walked slowly by, she took a quick but in-depth look at what was going on inside the private vault. Men were loading bricks of what she believed were gold bars, and one of the brothers and his daughter opened several lock boxes and poured out what looked like diamonds in five hand-sized black bags. This was way too exciting for Michelle, so she decided to stick around two hours after her shift was over just so she could see how the day ended. Jesus tried his luck once more with a last attempt to sway Michelle. He told her that if she was ever in the south of France or planned on visiting France, she would be more than welcome. He told her she would personally receive a royal welcome from him. Michelle smiled and asked Jesus if that offer would still stand if her boyfriend also came along. Jesus was caught off guard a bit by her statement and replied why would you bring sand to a luxury beach. He then kissed her hand and walked away smoothly, placing his Cartier sunglasses on his face. The family walked out of the bank at 4 pm with multiple bags. The word around the bank was they left with over seventy million dollars in cash and eighty million gold bars. Everyone in the bank was blown away that normal people could have that much money. Then, rumors started about who these men were. Michelle kept her mouth shut on what she knew and focused on what everyone else had to say. The main rumor Michelle was focused on was the rumor that seventy percent of the bank's money belonged to the Hernandez brothers and how they came to be so wealthy.

The Hernandez family stuck to their plan and quickly made their exit out of Colombia safely. Michelle walked home, thinking how charming and handsome Jesus was. She thought about the life he could possibly have offered her. She loved that he was Hispanic and living in a city she could only dream about visiting. She reflected on the fact that she had never left her home of Colombia since she was born. Every bone in her body wanted to take Jesus up on his offer to visit him in France. When she got home, her boyfriend was cooking dinner for her. She then came back to reality and smiled at what she did have. A handsome, loving man who worshiped the ground she walked on. She walked up to him and gave him a hug from behind. Her boyfriend Miguel turned around, kissed her, and smiled. He asked her to wash up because dinner would be ready in five minutes. She was already two hours late getting home to him.

Over dinner, the two laughed and talked about their day. Miguel told Michelle he planned to surprise her today by stopping by her job so the two could have lunch together until his uncle told him to make some unscheduled stops for his uncle's company. Michelle let him know it was okay because the bank was so busy, and the owner of the bank was there. The moment she said that Miguel's facial expression changed from smiling and happy to confused and unsure. Miguel asked her to repeat what she had just said to him again.

Miguel: Espere un minuto son usted me dice que los hermanos Hernández, los dueños originales de su banco fueron su hoy? (Wait a minute, are you telling me that the Hernandez brothers, the original owners of your bank, were there today?)

Michelle: Bebé sí, pero ¿por qué que molesta le? (Yes, baby, but why does that upset you?)

Miguel: Antes de decir otra michelle Contéstame a esto. ¿Es el hermano de Hernández todavía aquí en Cartagena? (Before you say another michelle answer me this. Are the Hernandez brothers still here in Cartagena?)

Michelle: Ningún bebé parecen salían hacia el aeropuerto. (No baby they look like they were leaving straight to the airport.)

Miguel: Dios de temor! ¿Sucedió algo como decir donde vinieron o donde ellos donde va? Vamos creo que Michelle, bebé de pensar. (Awe, God! Did they happen to say anything like where they came from or where they were going? Come on, Michelle, think, think, baby.)

Michelle: Sí, pero por qué es tan importante para usted? ¿Por qué están actuando de esta manera? Miguel hablar conmigo, me dice que esta mal, me dicen lo que está sucediendo de bebé. Usted me asustar! (Yes, but why is this so important to you? Why are you acting this way? Miguel talks to me, tells me what's wrong, tells me what's going on baby. You are scaring me!)

Miguel: No tengo tiempo para explicar, solo tienes que decirme lo que sabes ahora por su propio bien. (I don't have time to explain, you just need to tell me what you know now for your own good.)

Michelle: ¿Por mi propio bien? ¿Qué quieres decir con eso, es mi vida en peligro Miguel? ¿Qué es el no decirme? (For my own good? What do you mean by that, is my life in danger Miguel? What is it you're not telling me?)

Miguel then went to her side of the dinner table and grabbed Michelle from her seat. With a very firm hold on both of her arms, she shook her with extreme anger and continued to question her. Michelle had never seen this side of the man she loved so deeply. Everything about him seemed completely different. She didn't know this person she shared a bed with every night.

Miguel: Mujer ¿usted sólo responder a mis preguntas de mierda? (Woman would you just answer my fucking questions?)

Michelle then broke down from fear and told Miguel they were heading back to the South of

France, and that's all she really knew. Miguel then, looking more confused and unsure what to do with this information Miguel, simply jumped up, grabbed his shirt and shoes, and headed for the front door without a word to Michelle. As many times as Michelle asked him what was wrong, where he was heading, and why he was leaving, he refused to answer her. He didn't seem to care that she was frightened and was crying hysterically. He just walked out on her.
From the day Michelle met Miguel, it was love at first sight for the both of them. Miguel introduced Michelle to a more lavish lifestyle. After they moved in together, his uncle gave him more responsibility for his company. Their lavish lifestyle was way more than most people in Cartagena, Colombia, we'll ever know. For the past two years, Michelle only knew that Miguel worked for his uncle, who lives in Bogota. His uncle Emanuel was some kind of investor and international transporter who made millions. What Miguel did for his uncle she was really unclear of, and it didn't really matter to her either. As far as she knew, everyone in Colombia had some kind of history of unlawful business practice anyway. Even the law enforcement in Colombia was crooked.

Miguel raced out the front door, leaving Michelle crying and worried at the front door. He jumped into his classic Porsche 944 and raced down the street. He headed straight over to his father's house first. Miguel had to let his father know that the Hernandez brother was just here in Colombia and that they were indeed alive. Miguel was driving like a madman the whole way to his father's home. Miguel was in such disbelief that he crashed his Porsche into his father's front gate. He jumped out of the car with the engine still running. His father's guards ran to the front gate with their guns out because they thought someone was breaking in. Miguel ran past the guards into his father's home screaming for his dad. His father was upstairs in his master bedroom with two underage girls barely over sixteen years old. His father had one of the girls eating the other's vagina while he fucked her doggy style. Miguel's father heard him screaming and grabbed his robe downstairs. Miguel's father didn't take this news well. In fact, Miguel's father was a peaceful individual, and for years, he kept his hands clean from any bloodshed. Knowing the Hernandez brothers' whereabouts meant they would be going to war and bodies were about to pile up wherever they were. Miguel and his father video chat with Emanuel and updated him on this new situation.

Emanuel worked as an underboss for the Vasquez brothers for years. Emanuel came to power when the Vasquez brothers were all murdered. A part of him was extremely grateful to the Hernandez brothers for murdering his bosses. Emanuel had become extremely wealthy and was now his boss. He sat at the table with all the other cartel members now. Emanuel was very well informed on the situation between both parties, Vasquez brother and the Hernandez brother's history. The Cartel had an overwhelming belief that the Hernandez brothers orchestrated Vasquez's brother's death. The cartel issued a lifetime bounty on the Hernandez's heads. Even though Emanuel was grateful that the Hernandez's killed his bosses, he had to act on this information. If the five heads of cartel bosses ever found out he knew any form of information about the Hernandez's and did nothing, they would consider him unfit as a leader, and they would kill him as an example. He also knew something had to be done immediately.

Chapter Three
Burning Bridges

Ernesto invited my family and me down to see him at his home. Once we got there, he had five different party planners with him. He was planning on throwing a big, lavish, over-the-top party for no reason. I, myself, like to keep things very low-key these days. I drove a Lamborghini and my wife was driving around in a four-door Bentley but that was it. We had our home built from the ground up. It was a rather modern home. Seventy percent of our home was all bullet-proof one-way glass. Which meant I could see out, but no one could see inside my home. My wife referred to our home as a fortress instead of a mansion. I was so paranoid when building our home that I had our builder build a safe room with an escape elevator leading three stores down. I did not stop there at all. I spent another eleven million for a secret tunnel that was a mile-long route underground that led to a highway not far from our home. This tunnel was so my family could get away in case of any real danger. We had two fully bulletproof sport utility vehicles down there at all times. I also insisted that our family keep our family circle tight.

I was looking forward to seeing Ernesto and the family because it had been some months since I last saw Ernesto and we had a lot of catching up to do. I had spent the last two weeks closing a deal on a property I wanted to turn into a luxury five-star hotel in Nice. The timing was very right because I had paperwork in my pocket making Ernesto my partner on this deal. Now since Hernandez brothers and I needed to stay off everyone's radar, all our business dealings, property, and companies we own were set up in a few different shell companies in our children's real names. The cartel, feds, and anyone else looking for us never knew we had kids. We felt this was the best option to stay safe.

After Ernesto had laid out his grand plans for his party and we had discussed the hotel venture, I went home. I got home that afternoon and waited to tell Angelina that she and I would be taking a small helicopter ride to see her brother for the weekend. This made her extremely excited. Angelina was never away from my side for more than four hours in a day in twenty years. Our love and bond were just that strong. She was quick to start packing her luggage while calling Jax and Jaylyn on the phone. Our kids were away at school in Paris. The kids love being around their Uncle Ernesto and his kids. They always had a blast whenever they all came together. Jax was told to tell his real cousins Andrew Jr., my brother's son, Dane's son Carmelo, and Jamel's daughter Jenessa to fly out to Monaco with them for the party as well. All our kids attended the same university in Paris, costing me forty thousand euros per kid a year. I promised my cousin and brothers if they were to pass away before me and we ever had kids. I would give them the very best.

The kids were on the next private jet to Monaco with plans for shopping at every elegant store in Monaco before the party. The girls, Ana, Jenessa, and Jaylyn, once spent seven hundred thousand euros the last time they were all together, and I almost lost my damn mind. I guess they call that parenting and learning how to deal with the different characteristics of each kid. I did the smartest thing and booked three suites at the Hotel De Paris. If I made the kids do their own thing, I would die when I got the bill. I took them shopping, as stressful and painful as it could be. That way, everyone would stay within a certain budget. I was much more mindful of my money that day because I knew how fast it could go overnight. But nothing was more pleasureful than pleasing my kids.

Once Angelina and I landed on Ernesto's grand property in Monaco, we both smiled. We smiled at each other because Ernesto always had a way of outdoing himself with each and every party he hosted. The man had four all-white tigers in their cages to wow his guests. Women served half-naked in white European lace underwear, with small white sticks that just covered the women's nipples. They were servers for the night. Ernesto had about fifty beautiful women walking around with these stickers on their nipples in eight-inch red heels. Right outside of the main entrance of his twenty-plus bedroom home, Ernesto had ten of the most expensive cars in the world. All his cars had to be pearl white. Ernesto's cars were all on display as well. He had them all parked out front of his estate. Cars ranged from his Roll Royce black badge Cullinan, Ferrari 599 GTO, Lamborghini Aventador Roadster, Bugatti Veyron, his very rare Koenigsegg Agera. R, the Aston Martin One-77, and the list goes on. Whereas my wife and I would simply charter a helicopter for a quick trip, and we felt that was more economical. Ernesto, on the other hand, owned two luxurious helicopters with all the bells and whistles. Ernesto had to be the center of attention at all given times. I believe he got off on showing everyone in the room his bank book was bigger than everyone else. Only a few knew the truth about his financial situation, and we kept his secret. To my knowledge, Ernesto's funds were running dry, so something had changed because this party must have cost a few million euros. The party was filled with corporate morals, models, actors, and actresses. I was pretty sure eight
percent of these people didn't know who the hell Ernesto Hernandez was until that night. Nor did Ernesto care; he was more into just impressing people. Helicopters were landing one after the other for his outlandish party of his.

Ernesto: Awe, my favorite couple, my beautiful sister, and her ever-loving husband Paul.

Angelina: Hi, big brother; how are you, and where is Kimora?

Ernesto: I'm good little sister! Beautiful as always! Kimora is still getting ready, and it is 12:45. Please go up there and help her, sis. I need to talk to Paul anyway.

Paul: How is my good friend?

Ernesto: I'm great and absolutely stress-free.

Paul: Really now! Not to get into your business, Nesto, but the last time we spoke, you were worried about losing your home, and today, you're throwing a party that was to cost you a few euros well. So, help me fill in this puzzle here!

Ernesto: (Laughing) I just had to work something out, that's all. You worry too much Paul. Let me greet my guest and be a good host. Huel is over there with some people I need you to meet.

Paul: This conversation isn't over by a long shot, Ernesto. I have known you way too long, and I know when you're bullshitting me.

Huel: Paul, it's good to see you. I was talking to the Duchess and the Duke of Ireland. I was explaining to them that you're a hell of a businessman and you could possibly look over their portfolio.

Paul: It is a royal pleasure to meet both of your acquaintances.

Duke and Duchess: It's a pleasure also!

Huel: Paul owns a few luxury hotels, car dealerships, and even luxury yachts for sale or rental here in France. Paul's real passion has been the excellent wine company he acquired a year or so ago.

Duke: Wine? Now, Paul, you are talking my language. You must invite us to a tasting one of these days. I'm a great admirer of fine wine from all over the globe.

Paul: Well, we can surely make that happen. I'm looking for fresh feedback on the quality of my product. And you are surely a very lucky man. The duchess is absolutely radiant.

Duke: Why, thank you! They say the fifth time is a charm.

Paul: Fifth time you say!

Huel quickly caught on to Paul's surprise and before Paul could say something that would probably destroy the moment. Huel changed the subject.

Huel: So, Dutch, I would like to show you that Veyron supercar outside. Right this way, please!

I just laughed to myself, but the Duchess gave me that eye as if to say she would drink my offspring anytime I wanted her to. But that was my past life. If it weren't, she would be on her knees in the next fifteen with her lips around my dick. We took our exit from royalty and entered Ernesto's grand ballroom. Inside his grand ballroom was a table that could seat a hundred people, and there was food from one end to the other. He had huge ice sculptures in the middle of the room of himself. At each end of the room, there was a massive pyramid of champagne bottles. Everyone was wearing some form of white with a highlight of red, even myself. I had a way of feeling out of place at Ernesto's grand functions. I missed the old days with Dane, Jamel, and Andrew. To be honest, I wouldn't have been the same without them. I hadn't had to use a gun in over twenty years, but I never left home without one on my hip. I sent the kids to boxing and different martial arts forms for years. I needed my family to know how to defend themselves in case of anything. Huel and Ernesto made fun of my obsession for being so overprotective and somewhat paranoid at times. To me, being safe rather than sorry meant one more day on this earth, as far as I was concerned.

Huel and I had much to discuss, and he was always a straight shooter, and he didn't bullshit me like Ernesto would. I gave Huel twenty or so minutes more with the Duchess and Duke before he came and found me.

Paul: Anything new I should know about?

Huel: Nothing gets by you, does it? Are you asking where the money for these new cars and this very over-the-top party came from?

Paul: Bingo!

Huel: What I have to tell you, Paul, you can't lose your shit. Please don't become paranoid and overthink things. Ernesto and I took our kids to Colombia last week for less than a day.

Paul: What the fuck? Huel, are you fucking shitting me? Colombia! Colombia the country were the four of five major cartels want you two. Awe God!

Huel: The way you wouldn't lose your shit.

Paul: I didn't agree to shit.

Huel: Paul, we were damn near broke. I had two million dollars to my name. Once Ernesto had blown his money, well, you know mine was next. I'm sure Ernesto had less than thirty grand to his name.

Paul: That's because your fucking brother doesn't know how to stop spending money. We aren't drug dealers anymore. Did you two forget that? Save something for a rainy day.

Huel: Everything is ok, Paul; we went straight into our bank from the plane. Transfer our accounts into our kids' names and made a quick withdrawal from our accounts and took everything from our private vault, and then went straight back to our plane.

Paul: You had contact with someone for sure. That someone now knows the Hernandez brothers are alive.

Huel: The only person we interacted with was the bank manager at our bank. Paul, the manager, can be trusted without any doubt.

Paul: Trusted! The two of you put everyone in danger. I hope you know that. Fucking selfish!

Huel: Paul, we don't know if the cartel is even hunting for us anymore. We don't know if they even know who is responsible for the Vasquez brothers' murders. Paul, our family needed this. Ernesto would never take a dollar from you; he has way too much pride for that. His pride is way too big.

Paul: You guys, are you willing to find out? Isn't Huel serious? You and Ernesto put your kids, your beautiful wife, and your mother's life on the line. Not to mention my family as well. The cartel doesn't just kill you and Ernesto. They murder everything around you. Remember that. Cause you told me that, Huel, the day I met you.

Huel: We had no choice, Paul! It's something that had to be done.

Paul: Fuck you, fuck you, Huel, because I have over a hundred million dollars that I would happily give you two halves of that. Your fucking Spanish pride is going to get us all killed.

Huel: Paul, wait, Paul, wait, come back, Paul. Fuck!

With the news I had to ingest, I wasn't in the mood to party, drink, or enjoy myself. I was starting to think about moving far away from Ernesto and Huel for good. I knew this was something Angelina wouldn't like or want to deal with. What was I supposed to do? I couldn't lose anyone else, especially my kids. I wanted to leave the party immediately but looked at my kids' faces. The fun they were having held me frozen where I stood. Carmelo, Jax, and Jesus were hitting on everything with a pretty face, big breasts, and a tight dress. Angelina and I headed out around 2 am and headed back to the hotel. Angelina cuddled up next to me and wrapped her right leg over my legs. My wife started to kiss my face and neck. My body was numb. Angelina advised me that Ernesto and his wife were coming by for tea and brunch at our hotel in the afternoon. I wasn't up for that either, but I didn't want to worry Angelina about my paranoia, so I kept my mouth shut.

Chapter Four
Spark The Match

Angelina brought up this old guy who had too much to drink at the party. He started doing his best James Brown moves at the party. He even made sounds like James Brown. Angelina was laughing her head off, recapping one moment after another from the party. I kept looking behind us, and I told our driver to take only major roads back to the hotel. Exiting our car, I noticed a black BMW 750 parked across the street from our hotel. The same kind of Black BMW was at the heliport when we landed. The same kind of BMW was also outside when we left the hotel earlier. I mentioned it to my wife, and she assured me it wasn't. That there had to be a million BMWs and Mercedes in Monaco. From my hotel room, I kept my eye on the car. The car was so tinted black you couldn't see anything on the side at all. I couldn't tell if someone was even inside the car. But I could feel eyes watching us. I didn't say a word to Angelina as I slowly reached behind my dress coat. I reached for the gun holster on my belt and took my gun off the safety. I instructed my driver to leave the car where it was and accompany us inside. I walked behind my wife as we walked into the hotel. I used my body as a shield in case bullets started flying. To my surprise, nothing had taken place. We made it safely inside the hotel and to our room. Angelina was still running her mouth about the party when we got to our hotel room. I told my driver to watch over Angelina. I opened the door slowly and asked them to wait a second outside the room. She had this puzzled look on her face as I entered the room. The lights were off, and the room was dark. I pulled out my gun and quietly chambered a round. I took a moment to check each and every room in our suite. I was so damn relieved when I found no one inside our suite. I told the driver he could head out for the night but instructed him to be back early tomorrow to take us to the heliport.

Angelina sensed that something was seriously wrong. I was acting rather weird and more paranoid than usual. I closed all the drapes so no one could see inside. I told her it was nothing to worry about, but Angelina kept insisting I tell her what was wrong. Somehow, I couldn't bring myself to tell her. I didn't want to scare my wife or have her think I was weird and couldn't get past my history. Instead, I turned my full attention to my wife. I gave her what she loved more than anything. I lifted her up and carried her into the shower. She was still fully dressed in Chanel from head to toe. I didn't care. I placed her slowly on top of the bathroom counter. I kissed her and sucked on her lips and neck. She started undoing my belt buckle and pulling down my pants with her high heels. I ripped the back of her eight-thousand-dollar dress, and her mouth dropped. She slapped me one good time and then continued kissing me. She told me "You're replacing my dress tomorrow." I told her, "Whatever you want, baby." I lifted her dress over her head and threw it to the floor like trash. I ripped one corner of my wife's panties and then reached between her legs. She was so wet and hot. I could feel her pulsating in my hands. Her breathing became heavy and sexy. I pulled my wife's leg closer to my body, and she wrapped her legs around. I inserted myself inside her, and her body shivered. I picked up my wife and carried her into the shower. I made love to my wife in all different positions in that shower as the hot water washed our bodies. I loved feeling my wife's fresh, manicured nails pressing into my back. Her soft voice with that Spanish accent saying, "Fuck me, Papi."

Angelina religiously always moisturized her body after every shower. Just not tonight. No, my beautiful wife passed out in the hotel robe with her body still dripping wet. I pulled up the chair near the bed, enjoyed a glass of scotch, and watched her sleep for about an hour. Sitting in the dark across from her, I thought about the pain I would endure if I ever lost this woman. I picked up my cell phone and called my security team back home to meet me here at the hotel in the morning. I thought I was too paranoid or overly safe. I wanted my security to escort my family back home for all of our safety. I slept with one eye open all night, and I kept checking on the black BMW 750 outside all night. My gun never left the palm of my hand the whole night.

I kept changing hands whenever my hands started to sweat too much. Around 6 am the black BMW was gone, and to my surprise, the car never returned even up to the time Ernesto and Kimora arrived for lunch. My paranoia had calmed down a lot at that point, so I felt safe going out for lunch. During lunch, the ladies could pick up on the tension between Ernesto and me.

Waiter: Bon après Mesdames et Messieurs, je suis Jean-Perrie votre serveur et le brunch aujourd'hui nous servons un canard favorful, homard bleu de l'océan ou carré rôti od agneau. Si je peux donner temps de reflète votre choix que je peux commencer avec vos commandes. (Good afternoon, ladies and gentlemen, I am John-Perrie, your waiter and brunch today, we are serving a flavorful duck, blue ocean lobster, or roasted rack of lamb. If I can give time to reflect on your choice I can start with your orders.)

Paul: (Laughing) Would it at all be possible to repeat that in English, please?

Waiter: My deepest apologies.

Kimora: It's not a problem, sweetheart.

Waiter: Again, good afternoon, ladies and gentlemen. I am John-Perrie, your waiter. For brunch today, we are serving flavorful duck, blue ocean lobster, or roasted rack of lamb. If I can give you time to reflect on your choice, I can start with your orders.

Ernesto: Ladies, can I have the honor of ordering for you?

Kimora: Sure, Hun, or I'll be here all day trying to decide.

Angelina: Let's see if you still got it.

Ernesto: OK, we will start with a bottle of Petrus Pomerol 1998 or Dom. Romane Conti 1997.

Waiter: We have both sirs.

Ernesto: Well, bring them both, son.

Waiter: Will you be ready to order now or after your drinks?

Angelina: Now, would be fine, Hun!

Ernesto: OK, ok, my beautiful wife would love the brisk salad, and her main course will be blue ocean lobster. My gorgeous sister will have the Rivera salad and the blue ocean lobster as well. My uptight brother-in-law will have the duck, and I will indulge in the rack of lamb.

Waiter: It's my pleasure to serve you, and drinks will be out momentarily. Enjoy!

Kimora: Is there something going on between you two?

Angelina: Open your mouth and start talking one at a time.

Paul: I'm fine!

Angelina: Really!

Kimora: Ernesto!

Ernesto: What?

Kimora: You two have been acting weirdly towards each other all afternoon.

Ernesto: It's nothing serious, love.

Angelina: It better not be cause for two men in their forties; you two can act like damn children.

Paul: OK, let's just enjoy our meal; we can discuss private matters at another time.

Kimora: No, after this meal, you two will talk and clear the air.

Angelina: And solve whatever disagreement you two may have, period!

Ernesto and Paul: Yes, dear!

I couldn't wrap my finger around Ernesto and Huel's thought processes. Going to Colombia meant putting everyone in danger. Why couldn't they just understand that? There was no way they couldn't see that outcome. After lunch with the ladies, Ernesto and I took a walk around the beautiful hotel area, window shopping and basically burning off these calories from dessert and their European-rich coffees. I took that opportunity to get inside Ernesto's head.

Ernesto: I know you're mad! But you were able to leave the United States with more than half of your Riches Paul.

Paul: Yes, that's because I didn't put all my money into one bank. You forget I have about sixty million in your bank in Colombia. I thought of it as lost, gone forever. I'm kind of glad Dane wanted to spread our money around.

Ernesto: I had two hundred million in my Palm Beach home, hidden away before all the nonsense with the cartel. The cartel burnt my home to the ground before we left Vegas if you remember the day we killed those Vasquez's pigs.

Paul: More reason why going to Colombia was a crazy move. They burnt your home to the ground and destroyed your plane. Huel's home in California was burned to the ground also. Huel had six of his employees' bodies found in that house. They were all burnt alive.

Ernesto: Yes, I remember! It was all over every newspaper. Paul, those incidents took place weeks before we killed those Vasquez brothers. That was clearly what the Vasquez brothers were doing, not the cartels. I'm sorry, my friend, but a part of me had to know if I could get my money out. My money, Paul! The interest on that money alone is another twenty million since then.

Paul: You're like a brother to me, Ernesto, and I have lost way too much not to hand you fifty million dollars of my own money, Ernesto. No loan, all yours. You're worth more to me than money or gold.

Ernesto: You lost a lot, and I don't want you to lose anything else, especially what you and your family deserve.

Paul: We were stupid, Ernesto. I have lived with that pain over me every day. If my brother, my cousins, and I didn't want revenge for my parents' deaths. They would all still be here today.

Ernesto: We all played a part in that painful disaster.

Paul: I miss them!

Ernesto: I miss them also, bro.

Paul: Hold on a minute!

Ernesto: What's wrong?

Paul: I know there are thousands of BMW 750s in this city, but I have noticed one across the street for the past two days now. Don't turn around; just keep looking into the store. We can observe from the reflection of the store window.

Ernesto: They're leaving! Are you sure you're not just being paranoid?

Paul: Well, if your ass didn't just fly off to Colombia, where they are hunting us like dogs still to this day, I wouldn't be so damn paranoid.

Ernesto: (Laughing) I'm sorry, bro, but you should have seen your face just now. You tightened up like a virgin. That reminds me that I must call the bank manager in Colombia.

Paul: Is it wise for you to keep in contact with him?

Ernesto: I gave him an untraceable satellite phone that can't be traced back to me. I am not new to this. Paul, you forgot I taught you all the tricks of this trade.

Paul: Whatever!

Ernesto: When this call is over, Paul, I will burn all the untraceable phones. Is this up to your standards, Paul?

Paul: Make your call, you asshole.

Ernesto: No answer!

Paul: He didn't answer.

Ernesto: No, I do not like him to pick up.

Paul: Let's head back to the hotel. I need to boo, boo.

Ernesto: Nasty! You're the only person I know who shits after every meal.

We headed back to our hotel suite so I could poop and see the kids back off to Paris. Ernesto and his wife accompanied us back to the hotel. I love my kids and taking care of my brother's and my cousins' kids have been a blessing. My brother's ex-wife got remarried. She kept in touch with us a lot, which I loved. No matter what, she was family. After a few years of living in France with us, she returned to Atlanta with a whole new identity. Once a few years passed, we saw that she wasn't under any immediate threat. I even allowed Andrew to start spending summers and Christmas with her in Atlanta. Dane's first love, Javone, turned out to be nothing but an opportunist. A woman looking for a way out of Colombia by any means necessary. My wife let me know after Dane passed away that she had three kids in Colombia that her mother cared for. Her story was that she left them so she could follow her dreams. If she was able to do so, she was sure she would be able to better support her kids if her dreams came true. She and Angelina had a major fallout in the summer of 1998 when Angelina discovered that we were giving her ten thousand dollars every month to send to her kids in Colombia. Not a single dime of that money ever made it to the kids. Javone was heartless, and she kept every single penny. So, leaving her son Carmelo behind with us in France didn't seem to bother her one bit. It wasn't the first child she didn't care for. Angelina was heartbroken that her lifelong friendship with this woman was based on fraud.

I hated seeing the kids leave to go back to school. They were my world, and being a father was one of my greatest gifts. Once the kids left, the adults sat in the living room of my suite and enjoyed a glass of Louis XIII. We sat there for the next thirty minutes, just talking about life and our success before Ernesto and his wife decided to leave. Angelina and I walked to the balcony with our drinks to see them drive off.

I watch my dear friend Ernesto play the role of a gentleman by opening the car door for his wife.

He leaned over and gave her a kiss before walking to the driver's side of the car. Ernesto took a long last pull off his cigar before putting it out. He climbed into his beautiful baby blue two-door convertible Rolls Royce. He looked up at the balconies of the hotel, trying to find the location of my hotel room so he could wave goodbye to us. Ernesto screamed out to Angelina and me that he loved us. Before I could give my friend a mutual response, I noticed three black BMW 750s approaching. They were coming around the circle towards the hotel at top speed. At first notice, I thought to myself, there really are a lot of black BMWs in this city. Angelina was talking down to her brother, telling him we loved him too. I couldn't, for some reason, take my eyes off the black BMWs. Ernesto's cell phone rang as he entered the car, and we continued to watch to see them drive off. Then, my stomach tightened up, and I became frightened.

Ernesto: Mr. Ortiz, I'm glad you could find the damn time to call me back.

Person on the phone: Mr. Ortiz is dead, and so are you. Vaya con Dios. (go with God)

Ernesto looked at the phone and then at his wife with a scared look. I heard the tires of the BMW stretching. At that moment, my eyes closed to an incredibly bright light that came with a loud bomb. It was an explosion that knocked me and Angelina back into our hour hotel room and on our asses. We were both shaken up from the bast, and it took us a few moments to come to our senses. I asked Angelina if she was ok. My eyes were blurry, and my ears were ringing. Angelina was holding her head as if someone had just hit her with a baseball bat. I made my way back to the balcony as fast as I could. Ernesto's car had exploded into a ball of flames. The car was just burning, and people everywhere just stood by watching. The BMWs came at the burning car in both directions. One car from the front and one from the rear. Five men came out of both cars simultaneously. I noticed a list of different guns AK's: AR-15s and MPs. The men didn't hesitate to open fire with machine guns into the car that was already burning.

Angelina screamed out, "NOOOOOOO!" I didn't even realize she was standing next to me and looking down at her brother's burning car. The men from the third car opened fire at us on the balcony. I grabbed Angelina, and we fell back into the hotel room on our asses again. The windows are shattered into a million pieces, and the bullets riddled into the walls and ceiling. I told Angelina, "Baby, baby, I need you to grab your shoes and cell phone and forget everything else right now." With tears and fear in her eyes, she went to do just what I had told her to do. I grabbed my shoes also and my gun. I grabbed her by the hands and looked her in the eye. "Baby, when I say run, I need you to run; when I say down, I need you to get down. Ok! She was crying and so scared that I prayed she understood everything I was telling her.

I opened the door of our hotel room and looked outside to ensure it was safe. We started walking down the hallway towards the back, where the employee elevators are located. There were three housekeepers in the hallways and about eight guests as well. Everyone was on the ground, scared for their lives. I could hear multiple voices repeating quelqu'un de l'extérieur est en tournage. qui est en tournage ? Quelqu'un a-t-il mal ? (Someone outside is shooting. Who is shooting? Did anyone get hurt?) The two of us were speeding through the hallway. We were three doors away when the employee's only entrance door was on our floor. My gut told me the public elevator would lead us right into the armed men with machine guns. That's when the employee entrance door opened, and three men with masks walked out with machine guns. I saw my life flash before my eyes, but they were looking in the other direction at first. Which gave us three seconds to make some sort of move that could save our lives. A housekeeper had a guest room door open right next to us. With a quick reaction, I shoved Angelina into the room right before I heard "Ahí están" (there they go). I locked the door and quickly blocked it with a large chair next to it.

We were now locked in this room with this loud screaming and frightened housekeeper right outside the door. The housekeeper's scream seemed to get louder and louder with every second that went by. Within seconds, bullets started ripping through the walls and doors. I shoved Angelina's head down and led her into the bathroom. I locked her inside the bathroom for her safety. I can't say that I blamed her for all the screaming. With bullets flying through the air, filling the door with holes, the walls, and riddling the furniture in the room. Within seconds, everything inside the room was ripped to shreds. There wasn't anywhere else for us to go, and no way of getting out the front door without bullets flying in our direction. The men outside the room kicked the thick hotel door every time they stopped to reload their guns. I could hear them outside screaming at each other "alejarse, alejarse, que voy a disparar el pomo de la puerta y cerraduras. (Move away, move away, I'm going to shoot the doorknob off.) Once they stopped shooting, I thought to myself this is our chance. I grabbed the sheets off the bed quickly and tied one end to the balcony and the other end around Angelina. She looked at me as if I was weird or out of my damn mind. We had only seconds to do this. I was going to lower Angelina down to the floor below us.

Angelina: Paul, no, no, you can't be serious. I'm not going over that balcony.

Paul: Either you go, or we stay here and get a bullet in each of our heads. We have less than a second before they come in here. That door is riddled with bullets and won't be able to stop shit with a few more kicks.

I pretty much lifted my wife and tossed her over the balcony. There was enough sheet for her to reach the balcony below us. The door broke open, and luckily, the chair was there. The first guy tripped over the chair and fell to his face. The second guy raised his gun to shoot, but I beat him to the trigger. I fired two shots rapidly. The first bullet hit him in the shoulder, and the other one in his neck. I quickly tucked my gun away in the front on the waistline of my pants and jumped off the balcony. I grabbed hold of the sheet with one hand like I was in the James Bond movie. The damn sheet ripped before I could grab hold of my second hand, and I slipped and missed the sheet. I landed two floors down onto another balcony away from Angelina. Damn near broke every bone in my ass. I blacked out for a few seconds. I could hear Angelina screaming, "Oh my God, Paul, are you ok, baby? Are you ok?" Still on my back, I waved up to her as I slowly came around to my senses. "Yes," I told her. I got up on my feet but was still very dazed. Somewhat delirious, I told Angelina to jump down to me, and I would catch her. Angelina was way too afraid, and I could see it in her eyes. She shook her head now and backed away from the balcony. I didn't have time to fight with her or make her see common sense by jumping down on me. Instead, she told me to meet her on the next floor and screamed at her no. "Angelina, no, you have to jump," but it was too late. She took off running. I started taking gunfire from two floors above.

The balcony door was closed, and no one was in the room. I fired a round into the glass door that left a nasty crack in the window. I kicked the cracked glass door out that shuddered into a million small pieces. Glass was everywhere as I made my entrance into the now slippery hotel room. I ran toward the front door and made my way into the hallway. I had no idea which staircase I should run to meet Angelina. I didn't want to risk going to the wrong staircase and missing Angelina. I had no other alternative but to wait right where I was, hoping she would find me. I kept my eyes on both staircases, one each side of the hallway. When the north side staircase door opened, I started to run toward it very cautiously with my gun raised in case it wasn't Angelina. My heart skipped a few beats well when I saw Angelina walking through the doors. A huge smile of relief formed on my face immediately. Until I saw someone exiting the staircase behind her as well. My smile turned into a concerned frown, and I stopped running toward her. I was frozen where I stood from what I saw. It was a man dressed in black military tactical wear. He had a machine gun pointing at my wife's head. I was lost for words. This man was huge and very muscular. The lower portion of his face, from the nose down, was covered with something looking like a turtleneck. Angelina was crying, and I started to cry too. I cried because I didn't see any way out of this. I knew then that my wife and I were possibly going to die in this hallway. This man had a firm hold on the back of Angelina's neck. She couldn't even look down or left or right. His hold on her was so firm Angelina was walking on her toes. I could tell Angelina was in pain from the way this man was holding her neck. She had tears rolling down the side of her face. Everything around me slowed down instantly till it came to a brief stop. Angelina gave up all hope of making it out of there alive. I could read my wife's lips saying "I love you" repeatedly. Before I could reply to Angelina, I was watching her forehead open like a can of coke as bullets blew the front of my wife's face open. I watched her body fall face first, and I screamed at the top of my lungs, "Nooooooooooo!" Every single person in that hallway was trying to get to safety. Instantly people started screaming and running from the direction of this man who just killed my wife. This situation instantly saved my life for the moment. These frightened people ran into his line of fire. He couldn't get a clear shot at me, but he still opened fire. These men were cartel hitmen, for sure. They opened fire with no regard for innocent lives. He shot just about everyone in the hallway who stood in the way of trying to kill me.

I could feel the force of each bullet passing by my head and body. I made a run for it with my head down and took the first staircase with an exit that I saw. I ran down five flights and encountered three men dressed in tactical wear. They had their back to me, thank God. I was able to get the drop on each of them. I didn't shoot to injure any incident bystanders. I was shooting to kill. I was only aiming for their heads and chests if I got a clear shoot. I Dropped all three minutes in seconds before they even knew I was standing behind them. Then, I made it outside the hotel using the employee exit. Once I was outside, I could hear the sirens of police cars and ambulances getting close. I made my way to the east side corner of the hotel. I stuck my head out to see if any of the cartel goons were in front of the hotel. There were at least twelve of them, and they were heavily armed. I thought to myself, Paul, be patient, wait till you can see the police cars making their way to the hotel. I knew I needed that diversion to attempt an escape. I hid between two cars for a few moments. At that moment, several police cars were in view and making their way down the straightaway, which was in line with the hotel. The cartel's men opened heavy fire with no regard for anyone's life. The French police heading straight for the hotel had to make an emergency stop. Three of the police cars crashed into other parked cars from taking heavy fire. The officers in the other cars had to make an emergency exit from their cars. They weren't prepared for the firepower the cartel was using. A few police officers on foot were running towards the hotel as well. Twelve other heavily armed men exited the three black Mercedes Benz trucks west of the hotel. With high-powered machine guns, they wasted no time and opened fire on the crowd and the police. The police cars were being cut to shreds, not to mention the people and police in the streets. Bodies upon bodies were dropping at an outrageous rate. In my mind, I wanted the opportunity to murder every last one of these men.

It hurt my soul to see all these people dying, yet again because of me. I couldn't do anything to help anyone but myself. I dropped my head from disgust with tears in my eyes. I had one handgun and three bullets left. There wasn't anything I could do for these people. I had to go to my family. I saw a valet key box open and a red Ferrari FF sitting right in front of the hotel with the driver's door wide open. I put my head down and ran over to the key box. I looked over my shoulder twice before grabbing a bunch of keys in my hand. With all the excitement taking place, no one noticed me. I was about to jump into this Ferrari, not knowing if I had the right key in my hand. I was keeping my head down so no one could see me in the car. I dropped all the keys in the passenger seat. I just pressed start hoping I had the right key with me. The dash lights lit up, and that loud-powered Ferrari engine just roared when the engine started. I slammed the driver's door, switched the car in gear, and hit the accelerator.

The engine screamed, and the tired burned till the streets were filled with smoke. I spun the car into a perfect 360 and headed straight around that circle to exit the street. Two of the goons that exited from the same side entrance I made my escape from caught a view of me and opened fire. The back window of the Ferrari was shattered, and I could feel the glass hitting my face, but I was focused on the road ahead of me and to get away. The Ferrari went from zero to sixty in seconds. As I made my escape, I passed Ernesto's car, which was still burning, and my eyes started filling with even more tears. I was extremely heartbroken and burning in pain. I just lost two of the most important people in my life in a matter of seconds. But I still had to keep it together to save my kids. I typed in my son's cell phone number, and I could literally feel my heart racing in my hands. I kept uttering the words pick up, pick up, until I heard, "Hey Dad, what's up?" I started crying with the joy of hearing my son's voice.

Jax: Dad, what's wrong? Why are you crying?

Paul: I don't have time to explain right now; I need you to call all your cousins right now. I mean, right now, Jax, tell them not to get on their flights and go straight to the safe house.

Jax: Dad, are you serious right now? Where is Mom? Is she with you?

Paul: Boy, just do as I said. I'm on my way, please. Do as I say!

Jax: OK, ok!

Paul: I love you, son. I love you so much.

Jax: I love you, Dad!

Paul: Now call everyone, please!

Jax did just what I asked of him. Jax was already with Ana, Jaylyn, and Carmelo. Andrew had gotten on an earlier flight to visit his mother in Atlanta. Jesus was still at his father's house, and no one could get a hold of him on the phone. Everyone started panicking and arguing with each other about what to do about Jesus, Huel and their grandmother could not be reached. The dilemma was whether we should go straight to the safe house, go to Uncle Ernesto's house, and get everyone out, or follow Paul's direct instruction and go to the same house.

Jax: Guys, guys, listen, something has happened. Something is serious for my dad to send us to the safe house.

Jaylyn and Ana: What happened?

Jax: I have no idea, but my pops said not to get on our flight. He wanted us to head straight to the safe house. I've never heard my father so afraid.

Carmelo: Are you fucking with me right now?

Jax: Fuck no! He sounds like he was crying man. We need to do just what he asks of us now!

Ana: I'm calling my father and mother.

Jax: Cool! Carmelo call Jesus and Uncle Ernesto. Jaylyn, you call Grandma's house.

Carmelo: Nothing is going through, bro. It's like our phones are blocked or something. Something seriously isn't right.

Jax: The satellite phone is working, but everyone I'm trying to call just won't go through on their end. Let's just do what my pops said and head to the safe house.

Ana: I'm sorry, but fuck that. I am not leaving without my father, my mother, Jesus and the entire rest of our family. They are all at Uncle Ernesto's house.

Jax: My pops know what he is doing, and this is what he has been training us to deal with since we were fucking five years old.

Carmelo: Your father has always been paranoid. And borderline fucking crazy; I'm sorry, but Ana is right!

Jax: Are you fucking kidding me right now?

Carmelo: Are you telling me, Jax, that tomorrow we could wake up to find out everyone close to us is dead because we didn't do anything but cover our own asses? Could you seriously live with that, Jax?

Jaylyn: I'm sure my father has a plan, guys. I know he wouldn't call just us alone. He didn't want us to get on the plane for a good reason.

Ana: I'm going for my family, my mother, my father, my grandmother, and anyone else at that house. Sorry, cuz, do what you have to do, but I'm going.

Jax: OK, we don't have time for this with your hardheaded fools. This debate can take all day with nothing getting solved. Carmelo, take Ana with you and keep trying to call everyone's numbers. My sister and I will go and get a clean car and meet you at the house in twenty minutes. If you guys get there and no one is there, don't wait for us. Send me a text and say nothing more than, "It's a no-go." We'll head straight to the Port de Fontvielle. Whoever gets there first gets the yacht ready to sail.

Carmelo: Who would ever think we would have to use Uncle Paul's paranoid plan one day?

Going against their uncle and father's wishes, the kids decided to take matters into their own hands and try to round up as many family members as possible to take everyone with them to the safe house. Most of my family members look at my father as a wonderful, successful businessman with an overwhelming paranoid sickness. Now we were all thinking maybe he was always right, or maybe he was just testing us right now. Still, he sounded so afraid over the phone. Either way, getting our family members was the best choice to be made at this time.

Chapter Five
Run or Die

We got to a car dealership owned by one of my father's closest friends here in France. He trained us to go there, and they had two bulletproof Cadillac trucks parked in the back that belonged to us. The trucks were completely clean. Untraceable license plates and no navigation tracking. He gave each of the kids in the family these custom Escalade keys. Each of our keys operated all the safe cars my father had in eight different locations all over France. That's just what Jaylyn and I did once we got to the dealership. We didn't need to see or speak to anyone at the dealership. We each had the code stored in our cellphones to the rear gates of the dealership. Once our driver dropped us off, Jaylyn called the code from her cellphone, and the large black gates opened. We ran to the two black Cadillacs. We jumped into one of the Escalated ESV with the heaviest bulletproof doors. We wasted no time and headed to Uncle Ernesto's house. One Escalade behind the other, ripping through the streets. The trucks had these huge steal crash bars on the rear and front of the trucks, and we used them along the way. We spilt through small mini cars double parked on the street like butter. We must have taken out twenty-two scooters along the way.

Carmelo and Ana left our uncle's cars and his two drivers at the airport and took a cab instead. In case they were being followed, no one would expect them to come to the house in a cab. That wasn't Hernandez's way. The two were extremely nervous because they did not know what they were going to see the moment they walked into Ernesto's estate.

At that very moment, Jesus had just woken up from last night's big party at his father's Ernesto estate. He woke up to find three beautiful French women still in bed with him. The women were completely naked, including himself. Bottles of empty champagne everywhere, as well as women's undergarments. Jesus walked into his big grand bathroom to shower off last night's funk from his body. He turned on his music and started the shower. He sang about five and a half good songs before he left the shower. He looked in the mirror to check out his perfectly fit and muscular body. He wrapped a towel around his body and combed his wet hair. As Jesus exited the bathroom, he checked his cell phone and noticed he had twenty-two missed calls from his sister and his cousins. He smiled, thinking they wanted to hear all the dirty details with the French ladies. Jesus looked up the moment he walked out of his bathroom and back into his bedroom to find a well-dressed man in a suit. He was sitting rather comfortably on his bed, smoking a cigarette. A second man stood by the bedroom door in black military wear. The second man was holding a rather large machine gun with a silencer. The man on the bed blew perfect circles with the smoke from his cigarette. Jesus noticed that the man on the bed was holding a handgun as well with a silencer. Jesus froze for a moment. He was really taken off guard. His heart started to race instantly! Jesus thought he could run back into the bathroom and escape through the bathroom exit that led into the hallway. Right before Jesus could make a move, three other men walked up behind him from his bathroom. They were all wearing black military attire as well, along with ski masks covering their face. The masked men were aiming their machine guns at him. Jesus looked around the room again to notice a whole lot more that he didn't see the first time. There was blood on the floor, and three women in his bed were missing the other side of their heads. Jesus quickly realized that they were shot at point-blank range while they were all still asleep. One of the ladies was shot in the back of her head, and the other two were shot in the side of their heads. There wasn't anything Jesus could do to defend himself but stand there naked with his hands over his genitals. The guy in the suit spoke in a weird accent and introduced himself as Gunther.

Gunther: A good day! My name is Gunter. I'm Albanian, so excuse my accent. A man can smoke a single cigarette in twenty seconds with strong lungs. Did you know this? One of man's best and worst gifts to humanity. But I love the smoke; I love the cigarette. It calms me!

Jesus: (Scared to death) What the fuck are doing in my house, man?

Gunther: Well, I am here to completely eradicate your entire family from existence. So Goodbye, young man!

Carmelo and Ana pulled up out front of the estates to notice there were no security guards on the estate grounds. The two of them wasted no time and ran straight into the house. From Jesus' bedroom window, they could hear their cousin Jesus scream out, "No, please, no." Carmelo and Ana stopped dead in their tracks in fear for their cousin's safety. They both looked at each other hoping to hear something else from their cousin. They didn't hear another word or sound after that. The two of them hurried to their cousin's bedroom as fast as they could. Along the way, they were counting the bodies of the maids, butlers, cooks, security guards, and even their two dogs were dead. Once they got to their cousin's bedroom, they were fearful of what they would see. What they saw was the three naked women dead on his bed. The sheets were soaked in blood. Blood dripping from the bed to the floor. They slowly entered with caution, trying their best not to touch or step into any blood. In the walkway of their cousin's bathroom, they found Jesus's lifeless body. Ana's emotions quickly took control over here. Her tears turned into a cry. Her body shook before she collapsed to her knees. The five men who had just killed their cousin were on their way out of the estate, celebrating among themselves for a job well done. That's when they heard a woman scream from inside the estate. The men had a confused and lost look on their faces because they had swept every inch of the estate for any survivors.

Gunther: Someone else is in the home, find them, kill them, now go, go!

Carmelo grabbed Ana from behind and covered her mouth from continuing to scream. Carmelo and Ana couldn't believe what they were seeing. They couldn't believe what was going on. Their whole world just got flipped upside down. Jesus' body had countless bullet holes in his naked body. Carmelo hugged his sister for a moment to calm her down. Ana was crying hysterically. She could hardly breathe. She gasped for air a few times. Ana dropped to her knee, and Carmelo joined her. He told Ana softly they couldn't do anything to help him now. But the men who did this may still be here, and they could have heard you. So, they needed to go. Carmelo heard voices and ran to the bedroom door to look in the hallways. He heard something smash in the hallways. This confirmed Carmelo's notion that whoever killed everyone in the house was still here in the house. Carmelo ran back into the room and told Ana they needed to go now. Ana was crying her heart out from all the pain and hurt she was feeling. Ana had never endured such pain or even seen death firsthand before.

Ana: No, no. We need to stay here with him. We cannot leave him like this, Melo.

Carmelo: The killers are still here; I'm sure I heard someone. If we stay here, Ana, I'm sorry to say we'll be right next to Jesus. Please, Ana, let's go.

The moment they walked out of Jesus's bedroom. They saw three large men running towards them. They heard some weird language, and then the men opened. Ana screamed why are they shooting at us? They didn't really hear anything that sounded like loud gunshots. But everything around them started shattering into pieces. Carmelo and Ana just witness small, medium and large holes magically appear in the walls. Carmelo's reaction was "oh shit," and Ana's reaction was to scream her head off. Carmelo grabbed Ana's arm, and they raced down the hallway as fast as they could run with their heads down low. They made their way down the main staircase of the estate. As they got to the front door, they saw some extended SUVs parked outside the front of the property. Carmelo yells to Ana this way. Carmelo and Ana turned around and headed towards the library. They ended up being fired upon by the men who were outside the property as they ran past the rear of the estate. Ana yelled at her cousin, "Not through the kitchen; we need to go left and downstairs into the garage." Carmelo found that idea beautiful since there was a fleet of cars and bikes to hopefully get away in or on.

Once they got down into the garage, Carmelo locked the doors behind them and blocked it with whatever he could find. Then they ran into another problem. All the keys to the cars were kept in a wall-mounted safe. Neither one of them knew the combination to the safe. This formed a serious problem for the two of them because this was the only idea they came up with under fire and serious pressure. At that very moment, Jax and Jaylyn were racing towards Ernesto's estate since neither Carmelo nor Ana texted them on the satellite phone to say anything good or bad.

Carmelo: Now, what the fuck do we do? How do we get into the lockbox?

Ana: I have no idea right now!

Carmelo: You have got to stop crying, Ana. You don't want them to hear you and find us down here. OK!

Ana: OK, I'll try!

Carmelo: Maybe we can get out through the side door and make a run for it.

Ana: Oh no, Melo, that courtyard is outrageously too big. They will see us for sure. I don't want to get shot!

Carmelo: OK, ok! This is what we'll do, but we must move fast. We'll check all the cars that are open and see if the keys are in them.

Ana: Good idea!

Carmelo: You found anything yet?

Ana: Hello, no!

Carmelo: Holly shit Veyron has keys in it.

Ana: Carmelo, that car scares the shit out of me. No one is supposed to go that fast.

Carmelo: We are today! Get it cuz.

Once Carmelo turned the key and pressed the start button, you could feel the power of the W12 engine and all that horsepower revving in their seats. The adrenaline was racing through Carmelo's veins from the rush of driving this car and the situation they were in. Carmelo looked over at Ana with a smirk and stated he had always wanted to drive this car. The power of that engine alerted the four or so men hunting them in the house. The cartel hitmen each started shouting, "Dans le garage, ils sont dans le garage" (in the garage, they are in the garage). Carmelo closed his eyes for a moment before hitting the gas. The power that came out of that car the very instant the gas pedal was touched was unbelievable. The car's power completely destroyed the garage door ahead of them as they raced off the property. With bullets firing at them, Gunther raced to the top steps of the estate with his cell phone in hand. He made one call, and at a moment's notice, he had a helicopter picking him up. As they left the estate, Ana called Jax on the phone. She told him not to come to the house and for them to head straight to the meeting area. Ana wanted them to be ready to push off to go. Carmel and Ana raced through the city, then the mountains of Monaco. Carmelo maneuvered the Veyron around creeks, trucks, buses, and cars at outrageous speeds. Ten minutes or less after leaving the estate, they noticed a helicopter flying low and right behind them.

Ana: Is it me, or is that this helicopter flying really low?

Carmelo: Damn, Ana, I think it's following us. Look!

Carmelo hit five miles straight away and opened up the full power of the w12 engine in the Veyron. The Veyron speeds up to a hundred and seventy miles per hour in seconds. Making it almost impossible for the helicopter to keep up the speed to follow them. Especially since the helicopter was flying so low. Gunther was getting rather frustrated that he couldn't get a clean shot for the fifty-caliber sniper they had on board. Gunther knew just how difficult it was to even shoot a non-moving target with a sniper rifle from a bouncy helicopter. The pilot had no choice but to fly higher just so they had an aerial view of the whole location below. It also made it easier to track the car at such high speeds. Gunther fired a few rounds at the car with his handgun. He couldn't stop screaming at the pilot for not having a semi-automatic rifle on board the helicopter.

Ana: I think they gave up.

Carmelo: I seriously doubt that little cousin. At the speed we are going, it makes it hard for them to follow us. They haven't gone anywhere. Trust me, they are just flying higher.

Ana: So how are you going to shake them if they are in a helicopter? It's impossible then!

Carmelo: I got this, Ana, so don't you worry!

Ana: Jax, just text me back. They just got there.

Carmelo: To the yacht?

Ana: Yes! He won't leave without us, will he?

Carmelo: Not in a million years. So here is the plan, little cousin. We are about five minutes away at this speed. The next 15 kilometers, you and I will jump out of the car once we are in the city. We'll make a run for it into one of these big hotels right by the ocean docks. We will drop our coats and walk out separately through a side entrance. Ana, you will get us a cab that will take us the rest of the way. I'll walk out 30 seconds after you.

Ana: What about Uncle Ernesto's Veyron?

Carmelo: (Looking at Ana like she is crazy) Are you serious right now?

Ana: OK, I see that look!

Carmelo and Ana drove into the Hermitage Monte-Carlo hotel in downtown Monaco with tires screeching to a halt. The two jumped out, and Ana grabbed the car keys and ran over to the valet. At the same time, Carmelo was screaming out her name to come on. Ana quickly requested a valet ticket and handed the valet her keys.

Carmelo: What the hell are you doing, woman?

Ana: I love that car!

Carmelo: What?

Ana: You got to drive it. Am I going to get my opportunity to drive it too?

Carmelo: Awe God!

The two ran into the lobby, and Ana told Carmelo to follow her. She ran into the busy hotel gift shop and grabbed two T-shirts and hats. The line at the counter was five people, and they were really pressed for time. Ana cut the line and dropped a thousand euros on the counter, and said, "I'm paying for everyone's items, including my own, thanks." she held up the items and ran out of the store. Carmelo asked a few employees while running past them, "Where is the closest exit?". When no one answered, he started getting frustrated.

Carmelo: No one is fucking answering me. They all just looked at us like we were crazy.

The two of them stopped running, and Ana approached an employee who must have been a bellman and said in French, "Do you have a side entrance or exit to your hotel?" The employee reply Oui, nous le faisons à l'Ouest et le côté est du bâtiment. (Yes, we do it's on both the west and eastern side of the Hotel)

Carmelo: Frigging French!

Ana held up both of her hands, implying that she was smarter than Carmelo. She got the question answered. Ana smiled as the two of them headed over to the west side of the hotel and towards the exit while changing their shirts at the same time. Once they were inside the small hall to the exit, Carmelo stopped Ana as she was about to run outside into the open. He had to warn her to play it cool, to keep her head down and simply blend into their surroundings. Once they opened the door and took a step outside, the satellite phone started to ring.

Ana: It's not my cell; it's Uncle Paul's satellite phone that's ringing.

Carmelo: I thought Jax said he wasn't going to call us. Just for us to use text messaging to communicate.

Ana: Hello!

Carmelo: Who is it?

Ana: Oh my God, Uncle Paul. Where are you right? Are you alright? What's going on? Who are these people trying to kill us? When will we see you?

Carmelo: Damn, woman, can you allow the man a chance to answer just one of those questions before you ask him another question?

Paul: Ana, Ana, I have no time to answer any questions right now. Just listen and answer my questions quickly and with one-word answers.

Ana: OK, Uncle Paul!

Paul: Are you safe?

Ana: Yes!

Paul: Who is with you right now?

Ana: Carmelo.

Paul: Are you at the meet point?

Ana: No.

Paul: How far are you?

Ana: Five minutes or so!

Paul: Good, but move faster. Every second depends on it. Now listen, when you get to the meeting point, I want you to sink each satellite phone and your cell phone into the ocean before boarding the yacht. Do you understand?

Ana: Yes, understood!

Carmelo: What the hell is happening?

Ana: He just hung up! No goodbye or good luck!

Carmelo: OK, but is everything ok?

Ana: We basically have no time to waste, so we need a cab. I'll call you when I'm on the way.

Carmelo: OK, there is one over there, cuz. Let's get into this cab quickly.

Ana: To the port de. Et si vous nous pouvez obtenir leurs en trois minutes mal paye un cinq cents euros. (and if you can get us there in three minutes ill pay a five hundred euros)

Cab driver: Fuck cinq cents euros, accrochez-vous (Fuck five hundred euros, hold on)

Ana and Carmelo got in the right cab, an S4 Audi, and the cab driver drove like he was in a street race. He made it there in a little over three minutes, and Ana paid him five hundred euros. The two of them jumped out of the cab and raced to the dock where the yacht was located. Ana had to remind Carmelo to dump his phone.

Carmelo: Do I really have to? I paid fourteen hundred euros to have this phone a year earlier. Plus, all the videos and photos of all my ladies are on here.

Ana: Yes, let's go! Drop it, Melo.

Heartbroken about his phone, Carmelo and Ana jumped on the hundred-forty-foot yacht, where the captain and his two first mates helped them aboard the yacht. The captain asked the two of them, "If there is any chance, they could have been followed." Carmelo and Ana replied, "No, not a chance." The captain then informed the two of them that their cousins, along with their uncle Paul, were in the main suite on deck 2. The look on the captain's face wasn't too pleasing, which meant something was wrong.

As Carmelo and Ana walked into the main cabin, they saw Jaylyn and Jax sitting on both sides of the bed next to their father. Paul was shirtless and had bandages whipped around his shoulder and stomach. Ana and Carmelo rushed to their uncle's side as well with a deep concern for their beloved uncle.

Carmelo: Uncle Paul, what happened?

Paul: Awe my beautiful niece and handsome nephew, I'm glad your both safe. Your uncle will be ok, so don't you worry.

Jaylyn: (Crying) Dad was shot!

Paul: I guess I took two shots for a large caliber rifle.

Carmelo: How, where?

Jax: Ana, Jaylyn, please stop crying. My dad is strong; you guys just missed the doctor, and he assured us he'll be fine.

Ana: I don't know what's going on right now. People are dying all around us.

Jax: We believe the bullets came in from the rear of the Ferrari Dad was driving.

Carmelo: I didn't see any Ferrari when we got here.

Jax: Don't worry, we just dropped it at the bottom of the ocean. Dad took one shot that ripped through his shoulder, and the other grazed the meat and muscles from his back to his stomach. He was lucky the bullet missed all major organs.

Jaylyn: Where is Jesus?

Ana: Jesus didn't make it. He is dead. They murdered him. His body was just there, bleeding everywhere.

Jax: What?

Jaylyn: (Hugging Ana) It's ok, Ana, it's ok. We'll get these bastards to trust me.

Paul: (With tears in his eyes) No, no, you won't. No one is to do anything. You all will leave this alone. I will handle this!

Jax: But Dad!

Paul: Jax, no damn it! You will do nothing. Carmelo explained to me what happened and what you saw.

Carmelo: OK, uncle! When we got to the house, everyone was dead: the cooks, the guards, all the maids, those bastards even murdered the dogs. We found Jesus in his bedroom; he was fully naked, like he just got out of the shower. They shot him repeatedly, Uncle Paul. They shot him in the head; they shot him dead.

Jaylyn: No, no, this can't be happening to us.

Paul: Everyone, sit down. I have a lot to tell you guys. There is a lot you guys don't know about me, your fathers, and the life we once lived. The real reason why we are all so wealthy today.

Chapter Six
Family Ties

The kids did their best to get comfortable around Paul and embrace the next two hours of Paul's life story. Paul gave the children every detailed story of their family's past lives and why his wife, parents, brothers, cousins, Ernesto, and his entire family are dead today. The girls were overwhelmed and didn't take the news of all the deaths their family had caused well. Their lives, their worlds of luxury and glamour, are built on blood, lust for power, and countless deaths. Jax was the strongest of the group mentally from the devasting story his father just told. At the age of only twenty-two, he knew that his father's burden fell on him. His sister was only two minutes younger than him, and Ana and Carmelo were barely twenty-one. He had to take the lead on this. They left their uncle's bedroom to sleep once his story was over. The boys took eight bottles of gin and vodka from the bar in his bedroom. The kids took their conversation to the back deck of the yacht. The kids discussed everything they had learned. They weighed every option at hand. They knew Paul wanted his family to go into hiding until he was 100 percent better. Paul gave the captain detailed instructions to sail to England.

The kids spent the next few hours weighing their options: hide or find out which cartel was hunting them. Where would they even start looking? How and why was this happening to them after all this time? Where were Uncle Huel and Andrew, and were they still alive?

Ana: We must keep trying to reach both of them!

Jaylyn: We aren't going to England, so we can check with the captain to see if we have enough fuel to get to the United States. My dad had a list of fake passports made for each of us two years ago. We'll use those to keep our real names covered up.

Jax: Whoever these people are, they are well funded. High-power weapons, equipment, helicopters, and cars, and they don't give a fuck about collateral damage.

Carmelo: From what Uncle told us, they damn sure don't; they shoot up the whole Hotel de Paris and murdered countless police officers without caring.

Ana: We won't need weapons too!

Jaylyn: Ana, do you still think my father is a paranoid wreck?

Ana: I never said that! I said he's kind of crazy, and what's that got to do with weapons?

Jaylyn: (Smiling) Follow me, children.

Jax: You guys are going to love this. Seriously!

Jaylyn and Jax took their cousins down to the ship's cargo hold to show them all the toys and weapons their uncle had on board!

Jaylyn: My pops only showed us this because he knew everyone had started to talk about how crazy and paranoid he was. The safe car he told us about that Jax and I picked up is a Cadillac SUV with the extended cab fully armored.

Jax: It was reinforced steel throughout the truck and bullet-resistant glass capable of stopping up to fifty caliber rifle and bullet-resistant run-flat tires.

Jaylyn: Come inside the Escalades and check it out. The back seat opens up here, and you find three machine guns and a 45-millimeter Glock. Inside this hidden compartment in all the rear of the seats.

Jax: Dad only likes high-caliber quality firearms.

Carmelo: I'm impressed to the fifth power. Go, Uncle Paul! This shit is bad.

Jax: That's not all!

Ana: There is more?

Jax: Yes, the boat has tons of weapons on board as well RPG'S rockets, on the front and rear of the boat are four hidden fifty caliber mini guns with ten thousand rounds.

Carmelo: Wow, some real James Bond shit.

Jax: Yeah, you can say that again, but my pops prayed daily that we would never have to use any of this stuff. Carmelo, I know you have a sexual edge for horsepower. The truck has over seven hundred horses, and the engine is tuned with a supercharger. With a top speed of 160 miles per hour to pull that extra thousand pounds of steel.

Ana: I love how Uncle Paul upgraded everything on board the truck: the television, fridge, wine, and champagne cases. Really nice!

Carmelo: What about funds? We are going to need a lot of money to fund this James Bond mission.

Jaylyn: We have a little over ten million in bonds on board as well. All the bonds are written in Jax and my fake names on our American passports. We'll change out millions each at two different banks to stay under the radar.

Ana: If anything, we can always go into Colombia. My father and uncle have seven hundred million dollars. What if we just take that money and just disappear?

Carmelo: Colombia?

Jax: What do you mean Colombia?

Ana: Uncle Ernesto and my father took Jesus and me to Colombia a little over a week ago to transfer all their accounts and funds into Jesus's and my name in case anything ever happens to them.

Jaylyn: Ana, this is why everyone is dead. This is why this is happening to all of us.

Ana: I don't understand, guys!

Jax: You stepping foot in Colombia started a chain reaction. Someone saw you guys; someone said something to the wrong person. It can be a list of things, but here we are now.

Carmelo: They followed the paper trail back to us, is what you're saying. It's kinda of funny! Who knew we would be cleaning up our parents' mess? Jax, we can't run and hide from these people.

Ana: I don't think so, and we didn't say anything to anyone while we were in Colombia. Daddy strictly dealt with the bank manager only.

Jax: At this point, it doesn't matter!

Jaylyn: Maybe it does matter! Listen, if we can find the bank manager, tellers, guard and lean on them someone can tell us something.

Ana: Jesus was really friendly with this one pretty bank teller.

Carmelo, Jax, and Jaylyn (Looking at each other), "Jesus's big mouth!"

They called it a night after trying to reach Huel and Andrew for a few hours with no luck. It was the longest night for everyone cause no one could sleep. Everyone was too worried about what the outcome of this was going to be.

Andrew, with his dark sunglasses, was knocked out on his flight to Atlanta to visit his mother. He didn't turn back on his phone the entire flight. During the flight, Andrew was very uneasy about this one guy who didn't speak to anyone, and he had a very aggressive demeanor about himself. Andrew and this man kept exchanging dry eye contact. Andrew got up in the middle of the night and took a walk to the restroom on the flight. The strange Hispanic guy was the only person on the flight who was still awake. He didn't blink or break eye contact with Andrew, not even for a second. Andrew couldn't help but give this guy back dry and dirt looks. Andrew was about to let this man scare him or punk him.

The minute Andrew's plane landed in Atlanta, Georgia, he grabbed his Goyard duffle and exited the plane. He was glad his first-class seat was one of the first to exit before everyone else. Running into that guy again wasn't something Andrew wanted to do. The moment he turned on his cell phone, he had twenty-nine voicemails and thirty-four text messages. He pressed on his text message icon, and his cell phone instantly died. His car service was there to pick him up and take him to his mother's house in Alpharetta, Georgia. Halfway he realized he didn't bring a single thing for his mother and two little sisters. He told the driver to stop off at Lenox Mall to do some shopping for them.

He ran inside and went straight to the Louis Vuitton store and purchased his mother two handbags with matching wallets. He got sneakers for his little sisters from the Gucci store. Andrew took a few moments to himself and indulged in some of his favorite watches. He picked out a nice 18kt gold Hublot Big Bang Chronograph as a gift to himself. While standing at the check-out counter and waiting for the cashier to process his purchase, Andrew looked past her and into the mirror behind her. He saw the same Hispanic guy walk right past the store and look straight at him. The guy was wearing black leather gloves and clinching his fist rather tightly. This sent an uneasy feeling straight down Andrew's spine and into his Andrew's guts. Andrew asked the cashier if they had a side exit to the stores. She said no, only a rear exit for employees. With the amount of money Andrew had, he handed it to the cashier and pointed to the exit, implying to her he wanted to use the exit. She couldn't tell him no. As Andrew walked towards the exit, he tried to call the driver to meet him outside the mall immediately.

Andrew looked both ways before he made his exit. The cashier grabbed his wrist and turned around to acknowledge her. The beautiful cashier looked him straight in the eyes, and with a sexy smile, she handed him her phone number. He smiled back at her and bit his bottom lip to let her know he was so interested in getting to know her, just not at this moment. Andrew looked both ways again and started walking very fast toward the exit. He kept looking behind to see if this man was coming. The third time he looked back, the Hispanic guy had company. There were three other Hispanic guys, and one of them was huge. The relatively huge individual looked scary, with scars all over his face. The moment they pointed in Andrew's direction, Andrew knew for sure this was no coincidence. With no hesitation, he turned and began to run as fast as he could out of that mall. Andrew was a high school track star, but his adrenaline was pumping. This wasn't a track meet cause Andrew was frightened. Andrew saw the exit door to the mall and felt relief. He had a large distance between himself and the men pursuing him when he heard three gunshots extremely close to his body. He turned to look back, and the men were shooting at him. Andrew thought to himself, "holy shit." He grabbed the handle on the door and made his way outside of the mall. He continued to run in a panic as he scrambled for his cell phone to call his driver. He asked the driver repeatedly, "Where are you?" The men pursued him through the crowded parking lot of Lenox Mall. His car was just pulling up to the entrance of the mall. Andrew ran past oncoming cars that just missed hitting him. Andrew opened the rear door of the car and jumped inside. Before the rear door could close, Andrew was screaming at the driver, "Go, go, go!" Andrew looked in the rear window to see the four men running blindly into the middle of the street with guns in their hands. At the microsecond, the four men caused a major three-car accident. The cars all ran into each other not to hit the four men. The men didn't jump, turn, or react to the accident that could have taken their lives. They were only focused on the SUV I was in, which was now out of their reach.

Andrew was extremely happy to be home at his mother's, and he couldn't wait to tell her what a day he'd had. He tipped the driver big, then walked inside the house, dropped his bag, and plugged his phone into charge. He didn't wait to see that Apple symbol pop up on the screen. He just headed downstairs to hang out with his family.

His mother and sisters were extremely excited to see him. His sisters were more excited about the expensive gifts he always brought them. Andrew greeted his stepfather with a handshake. After having a great dinner his mother prepared and tons of laughter and hugs, Andrew went upstairs to shower. After his shower, he checked his phone and saw all the text messages from his cousins. The last message he got was, "Andrew, I pray you're alive, and we can't tell you where we are because our lives depend on it, but we love you. He decided not to check any more messages and called his cousins right away.

Andrew: Hello Ana!

Ana: Oh my God! Andrew, I never thought I would be so happy to hear your voice.

Andrew: Thank you. What the hell is going on?

Ana: Hold on.

Jax: Hello Andrew!

Andrew: Yeah, I'm here, what's up?

Jax: There isn't any nice or comfortable way to break this news to you, but almost everyone we love is dead.

Andrew: Dead. Who is the dead, man? Cause if this is some kind of joke, I'm not laughing, Jax. Not after the day I just had.

Jax: Listen, listen, Uncle Ernesto, his wife, Jesus, and my mother are all gone. My father is laid up with two bullet holes in him.

Andrew: Are you shitting me? Please tell me your fucking with me. I had four Hispanic cats chase me through the mall today with guns. One of the guys was on my flight, and I knew something was wrong from his whole demeanor.

Jax: Cousin, you got to keep moving. You can't stay wherever you are. If you're at your mother's, get them out of there. I believe these people are tracking every one of us. We haven't heard from Uncle Huel yet. If they were on your flight, chances are they know where you are, and you can't take that chance, so get out of that house and keep moving.

OK, I'm going to get the girls up right now, including my mom. What's going on?

Just then, Andrew heard glass being smashed downstairs while he was getting his mother to pack up herself and his sisters. He then heard his stepfather's voice, "Who the hell are you, and what are you…" Andrew knew his stepfather didn't get the chance to finish his sentence, and right away, he heard another smashing sound. To him, it sounded as if someone's body just hit the floor. He told his mother and sisters to stay in her bedroom and to be very quiet. At that moment, all the lights in the house went out, and the home was completely darkness. He knew he had seconds, not minutes, to get his family out of that house. He asked his mother for the car keys to the truck he had bought her for Christmas. His mother told him that the keys were in the garage, along with the other car keys. Andrews's mother and sisters were crying. They were so afraid. Andrew told them to make their way outside the girl's bedroom window and down the storm drain. He was going to try and make his way to the garage without getting himself killed. He instructed the girls and his mother to run to the track, race to the gas station, and take the back trail behind the house as a precaution. He told them to keep their phones switched on. He threw a glass cup across the hallway as a diversion to buy his family some time. He sent the men into an empty room while the ladies made their way out the window. He witnessed the four men investigate the noise, wearing night vision goggles. Andrew quietly made his way around them and down the back staircase of the house while they were busy searching the room in which he had thrown the glass.

It was rather difficult for Andrew to find the door in the dark as he made his way downstairs through the den and kitchen. He could hear the men upstairs check room by room for him and his family. He looked for his stepfather in the dark and saw an object of a body on the floor. Andrew knew he couldn't risk the safety of his moms and sister if he tried to save his sister's father. Andrew made the biggest mistake ever, hustling through the kitchen. He knocked a pot off the stove right before he walked into the garage, and he heard one of the men shout in Spanish, "Downstairs." The men raced downstairs. Andrew ran into the garage and locked the door behind himself. He was in more trouble than he had hoped for. The lights being out was such a problem. Andrew had no idea where to look for the keys. During this whole situation, Andrew was undergoing. Jax was still on the phone, listening, praying, and hoping for his cousin's safety. Andrew started panicking, and he could hear a very low voice. He looked down into his hand and noticed his phone was still on, and Jax was on the other end. Which also reminded him that his phone had a flashlight. He told Jax to hold on as he used the flashlight to look for the keys. The flashlight was good and bad for Andrew. The men saw the movement in the garage because of the flashlight. They didn't wait. They just opened fire into the garage. Andrew couldn't hear any loud gunfire, but multiple bullet holes came flying through the garage door. All the walls and items inside the garage were getting shot to shit. Andrew fell on his back, and the light from the phone shone straight up. Now, looking straight up, Andrew saw a small shiny box on the wall. He thought to himself, that's where the keys had to be. Andrew crawled over to the box and ripped the box from the wall. He reached inside the box and grabbed every key in the box. He started pressing alarm buttons until he heard the Porsche's truck alarm go off. The moment the shooting stopped, Andrew could hear his heart beating. He had to take a moment to grasp his thoughts and convince himself to get up and get out of there. He climbed in the Porsche truck and started it up. He was glad to feel that six-hundred-plus horsepower engine roar.

Andrew didn't think for a second; he just hit the gas right before what was left of the garage door to the house got kicked down. Andrew didn't wait for the motorized garage door to open, either. Instead, he just drove right through it, rolling over everything in his path to get to his family. He paid no mind to the back windows being shot out as he made his getaway.

Andrew's family was safe but scared, and they patiently waited for him at the gas station. With every minute that went by, his mother watched her phone. His sisters couldn't stop crying. His mother had no problem cursing out anyone walking in or out of the gas station or whoever just looked at them wrong for standing there crying and holding on to one another. After five minutes, Andrew's mother decided to call the police. Before she could get four words out, Andrew came flying into the gas station. He hopped out of the truck quickly and told his family. "We have no time. Get in, get in." Once they pulled out of the gas station and, on the highway, Andrew called his cousins back. Jax answered with such relief, knowing his cousin was safe and alive. Jaxon instructed Andrew to head north on Highway 85 and to memorize the number he called Jaxon on. Jaxon wanted Andrew to dispose of the phone he was using as well as his family's phones. The first stop for gas was in South Carolina, where Andrew purchased two prepaid phones.

His mother waited till the girls were finely calm and asleep in the backseat before she asked a question she had already known the answer to. Was her husband alive or dead? Andrew just looked into the rear-view mirror, looking at his two beautiful little sisters, and shook his head no. The tears started to run down his mother's face from the pain of confirming the truth. Andrew called back the number from his prepaid phone.

Andrew: Jax, that's you?

Jax: It's me, cuz. How are you holding up? Are your mother and sisters, ok?

Andrew: Yeah, they are fine! They are cuddled up in the back seat. What's going on Jax? Cause I'm scared to death, man!

Jax: I can't explain in detail cuz, but it has something to do with all of our fathers back in the day when they were young, wild, and getting rich.

Andrew: What the hell are you talking about right now?

Jax: Cuz, why do you think my pops was always so hard on us growing up? All this combat training shit he put us threw. It's so we were ready to deal with this situation if it came to our front door.

Andrew: Yo! Jax, I almost got my head shot off, my mother and sister almost died as well, and you're not making any fucking sense to me right now.

Jax: Okay, head north towards New York. Andrew, you have to follow these directions to the T.

Andrew: OK!

Jax: Drop off your mother and sister at a hotel in Baltimore, Maryland. One of my dad's old partners, Basil, lives out there. He'll put the hotel suite with bodyguards under an alias name.

Andrew: The funny dude from Brooklyn that visits us every summer with Rob and their families.

Jax: Bingo! I'm reaching out to him; he'll keep them safe. Give Basil whatever credit cards, bank cards, and all your identification, and give your real names to no one. Because nothing can be traced back to you. Once you get there, get rid of that car you're driving. I'll have Basil take care of the car and get you a new one.

Andrew: So where am I driving after that?

Jax: You will be meeting us in Bay Shore, Long Island.

Andrew: I was thinking I would be meeting you at an airport or something.

Jax: Nah! We are on that yacht my father bought a few years back and customized it damn near military style over the years.

Andrew: Smart, real smart!

Jax: OK, I have to go. You be good, cuz, because we'll see you in two days.

Jax felt everything was set in motion now. He and his cousins knew it wouldn't take long before his father realized they had been at sea way too long. They had to convince Paul to see things their way and allow them to help him resolve this detrimental problem for good.

Jax took it upon himself the following morning to wake up early, prepare breakfast for his father, and help him change his bandages. When Jax walked into his father's room, Paul was already up and attempting to change his bandages.

Jax: Mr. Independent, good morning!

Paul: Good morning, son!

Jax: Did you sleep well at all pops?

Paul: Pretty much; nothing like having your body rock to the rhyme of the ocean as you sleep. I need to talk to the captain because we should have docked hours ago.

Jax: Let me help you with that, Dad. I made you breakfast as well.

Paul: (Laughing) What do you want to talk about? This must be important!

Jax: What do you mean, Dad?

Paul: You're my son now for what twenty-one years. I know when you want something or you need to tell me something, so you butter me up first.

Jax: (Smiling) Real funny, Dad!

Paul: What's on your mind, son?

Jax: This whole situation! I don't see how you are going to handle this on your own. These people are hunting us all like sheep.

Paul: I don't want you guys involved in this. This is my mess and mine alone.

Jax: Is it really Dad? Come on, do I have to spell it out for you? Dad, Mom is dead. She is gone. She is never coming back! My last words to her weren't I love you. I didn't get to say goodbye. Neither did Carmelo, Ana, or your little Jaylyn. Uncle Ernesto and his wife are dead, too, Dad. Jesus is gone!

Paul: (Screaming) You don't think I know that! You don't think this weighs down on my heart. I won't; I won't lose another person, another loved one, or anyone close to me. I'll be damn Jax!

Jax: So, what? We sit on the sideline, waiting, hoping these people don't find us.

Paul: You, your sister, and your cousin are not to get involved.

Carmelo: Sorry to interrupt Uncle Paul, but I see you're all bandaged up. The doctor said it would be anywhere from three to six weeks before you recover. The bullet almost ripped your shoulder off. Your shoulder may never be the same.

Jaylyn: You guys talk way too loud, but Dad, they are right.

Jax: If we sit and wait this out for six weeks, they may find us before you are fully recovered.

Ana: Not to mention, I won't sit around Uncle Paul. I don't know if my father is dead or alive. I can't get a hold of him through email, text, or on either of his cell phones. I'm sorry, but I won't sit around and wait. Once this boat docks, I'm going to find my father and get some answers to this situation. A situation we are all in!

Jax: Dad, you had us train for this situation right here 'cause you knew the problem with the cartel wasn't never really over, right? Dad, think about it; we have the element of surprise 'cause they don't know what we are capable of.

Paul: Do you kids know what it is to bury your whole family because of your foolish pride? Do any of you know? It's me that can't wash their blood from my hands. It's me who has to live each day with guilt. I can't do it again! I won't do it anymore.

Jaylyn: Dad, this problem isn't going away. Last night, Andrew and his family were almost murdered. Andrews's stepfather is dead, Dad.

Carmelo: This is way past your decision and your wishes, Uncle Paul. These people aren't playing by your rules.

Paul: Everyone get out, get out now!

Jaylyn: You know we are right, Dad.

Paul needed time to reflect on the issue and the kid's proposal to help him. He just couldn't process putting his kids in a situation like he did his brother and cousins in harm's way again. The kids had their minds already made up.

Andrew reached Baltimore after driving all night long. He reached out to Basil at a rendezvous point by the harbor. Basil had three large black dudes awaiting their arrival at the Baltimore Marriott by the downtown harbor. Basil had three rooms paid for. A room for Andrews's mother, his sisters, and two bodyguards to watch out for them for the next three weeks.

Basil: Oh my God, look at this handsome devil here. You look just like your father, Andrew. I miss him so much.

Andrew: Thank you, Basil! This is my mother and sisters.

Basil: Ladies, it is an extreme pleasure to meet you. Guys take the ladies to their rooms to clean up and get something to eat. Girls, this hotel has delicious French toast and, later, maybe some chocolate ice cream.

The girls: Yes, please! That sounds amazing.

Basil: You're in good hands, ladies. I'll talk to your son for a few minutes if that is okay with you.

Andrew: I'll be up there in a few minutes, Mom.

Basil: Listen, your old man, as you know, and I go way back. So, whatever you need, I am here for you. Those are two of my most loyal guys. They are both military black operations trained, and they won't leave your family's side for anything. I'll come and check up on them every night while you're gone. Jax told me you needed a car, something quick and low-key. So, I got you some American muscle.

Andrew: Thanks a lot, Basil; they mean the world to man.

Basil: They are safe with me, Drew. Damn, that's what we called your pops back then.

Andrew: I'm cool with "Drew." I like it. But you know I hate American cars!

Basil: Listen to you! You know beggars can't be choosy, right? Don't knock it till you try it. It's one of those new Chevy Camaro ZL1. 6.2-liter v8 supercharger, my young friend.

Andrew: (Laughing) We'll talk cars later.

Basil: (Laughing) OK, I spoke to Rob. He is in Miami, and between the two of us, we'll look into a few things for you. Andrew, if this is the cartel behind this, you can't trust anyone. The cartel won't spare a dime for any information on you and your family for your heads.

Andrew: Duly noted, Basil!

Basil: Go shower, eat, and say goodbye to your family. Oh, there is ten grand and a Glock 9 in the glove compartment.

Andrew: (Walking away) I appreciate everything, Basil.

Paul took a long, hot shower with his shoulder and ribs wrapped up. He reflected on everything that had taken place over twenty-plus years. He shed tears of pain before he got dressed and went down to have dinner with his family in the main dining area. When Paul arrived, the kids were already eating dinner. Paul sat down and greeted his family. For the first ten minutes, everyone was quiet after they said grace. Finally, Paul spoke, and everyone listened closely.

Paul: If you kids have made up your minds about this, I guess I can't stop you, and realistically speaking, I will need your help. If we do this, you all will have to listen and follow my detailed instructions on what to do. No questions, you do as I say, no questions.

Everyone just shook their heads in complete understanding of Paul's instruction. They then told Paul that the yacht was heading to New York to pick up Andrew, and they got in touch with Basil and Rob. Basil and Rob were using their contacts in Mexico and Colombia to find any information on who and why this was happening to them.

Paul: So far, you guys are doing well. Has either of them gotten back to you yet?

Ana: No, not yet, but Basil provided safety for Andrews's family in Baltimore.

Paul: Only men I trust beside everyone sitting at this table.

Chapter Seven
All Or Nothing

The next afternoon, the yacht docked in Long Island, and the whole immigration process was a lot easier than we had thought it would ever be. Especially when you can hand someone a hundred grand to look the other way and not ask any questions. They didn't even take the time to search the yacht at sea or when we docked. Andrew was parked about half a mile away, just sitting in the car and waiting for us to get there and call him. After we touched base, he met up with us at the docks. The captain told us they would need a few hours to refuel the yacht and get supplies to restock the food pantry. He said that he would be sending out two people to get this all done. I also picked up some burner phones. The captain was an ex-marine and really knew his shit. I asked Ana to accompany one of the two mates to keep an eye on them. I didn't trust anyone at all at this point.

Well, the immigration police walked the yacht. I had a beer with my father on the rear lower level of the yacht. He told me stories of my mother, how they had met, and how she meant the world to him. Then he hit me with the million-dollar question. Was I or any one of us ready and able to take someone's life? I told my father, "All I need to think about is that they are responsible for my mother's death." So, I wouldn't second guess killing every one of these bastards.

He placed his half bottle of beer on the ledge of the yacht, turned, and walked away without saying a word. I don't know if he was happy with my answer or disappointed. He honestly didn't even look at me. Once Ana, the two first mates, returned with supplies, we set sail immediately. My father remained in his quarters for the remainder of the night. He never left his room after that. He just laid in there with the light off. No television, no phone, no communication at all. Jaylyn checked on him a few times during the afternoon, and she was pretty sure she heard him crying. Her heart was broken because she knew he was blaming himself for everything that had happened. All his life experiences, preparation, and training had failed him. He was hurting in the worst way. Jaylyn just made a U-turn and headed back to her brother and cousins. She didn't utter a word to anyone but me about our dad.

Andrew and Carmelo returned shortly after Ana returned with their supplies. We didn't waste any time loading all the goods on boards and heading back to the seas. I asked the guy if "Everything went well," and all I got was a witty remark from Carmelo stating, "It's just groceries," I called Rob in Florida to touch base with him to see if there was any news on our current development.

Jax: Hey Rob, it's Jax. How are you, man?

Rob: (Laughing) How are you, kid?

Jax: I can't call it. Doing my best to keep our heads above water, bro. Honestly, we've all seen better days, you know.

Rob: My heart goes out to you and your family, kid.

Jax: I really hope I'm not calling too late.

Rob: Nah, man, for you guys, any time and anything. How is your father holding up?

Jax: Honestly, I don't know where his head is right now. This hit us all really hard, and we haven't even taken time to grieve over anyone in our family. Everyone pretty much got to man up and put that pain and hurt aside for now.

Rob: Your father is one the most loyal and strongest person I know. I would give that man first born if he asked. Your father doesn't handle personal death well, Jax. He took the death of his brother, and his cousins really hard. They were all inseparable growing up. You and your sister were way too young at the time to remember them.

Jax: I know, Rob. He never stopped talking about them, so I know he loved them dearly. Anyway, Rob, I have to keep this kind of short. Is there any word on who is behind all this?

Rob: Call everyone into the room and put me on speakers, Jax. Everyone is going to need to hear this.

Jax: OK, hold on!

I jumped on the yacht's P.A. system and called everyone down to my room. Once everyone was present informed them that Rob had some information he wanted to share with everyone.

Jax: Rob's on the line, and he wants to talk to everyone, so I put it on speaker.

Rob: Good day, family! I know it's been a good while since I've spoken or seen any of you guys. I'm extremely sorry, but it's under these circumstances. How is everyone holding up?

Carmelo: We are all trying to keep our heads. It's not easy!

Andrew: We straight, Rob! We just want answers at this point.

Rob: First, I'm not in Miami these days; I'm in Jacksonville. Things in Miami have been kind of crazy since the 80s and 90s, and I have learned to stay low-key the older I get. I'm a behind-the-scenes man these days.

Jaylyn: OK!

Rob: Since my days with each of your Fathers, Colombians aren't the main source suppliers of cocaine or heroin anymore. Now, you have to go through a Mexican cartel, pretty much. Bolivia at this point isn't on anyone's radar. Mexico is where you have to go. It was a lot cheaper and much easier in those days. The Mexican pipeline to Florida is tricky, and we lose one out of every ten loads. Because of it, every Mexican cartel has been at war for years over the drug trade. Every year, there's a new Mexican cartel popping up. The cartel bosses are getting younger and younger taking over their family businesses and branching out with their own cartels. There is a guy in Miami now and he goes by La Serpiente (the Snake). He heads one of the notorious Mexican cartels in the southeast region. I got in contact with his people, but to be honest, I don't trust them. Nor do I think it was a wise idea to do any kind of business with these people. They are straight killers and murderers. They are known for murdering women and kids with no remorse. A group of cold-blooded four-foot men with a Napoleon complex. But if I wanted to stay in business, I had no choice but to do business with them. They literally operate like a corporation. They demanded a five-year deal with me. Which entailed me purchasing a minimum of a hundred keys per month. I relocated further north to Jacksonville 'cause the drugs move faster here than in Miami. Crack that is! These boys out here re-up every other day, and I wholesale, so I'm pretty much supplying every dealer here. More importantly, no one knows who I am. I'm Robert Harris, your local neighborhood car dealer.

Carmelo, Andrew, Jax, and Ana (Laughed)

Rob: Don't laugh, kids. I'm serious. Some days, I feel more like a used car dealer than a drug dealer these days.

Jaylyn: They know. We just find you funny since we were kids.

Rob: Kids, I spend my days at the dealership, playing it safe. I have a lieutenant who handles my day to street business, someone I brought down here from New York. He is trustworthy and loyal. Anyway, let's get back to what I'm telling you guys. If anyone knows what happened to your family in Europe, it is this guy, The Snake. He will have the 411.

Jax: So, Miami is our destination then?

Rob: I'll meet you guys out there tomorrow afternoon. Please don't do anything until I get out there. One more thing!

Jaylyn: What's that?

Rob: There is a five-million-dollar bounty on each of your heads.

Jax: Fuck!

Carmelo: Are you fucking serious?

Rob: Yes, I'm fucking serious! They want Paul so bad that his bounty is fifty million dead, seventy-five million alive. So, I cannot express my desire to stay out of sight until I get there.

Jax: Don't take this the wrong way, Rob. But how are we supposed to trust you knowing you can get rich by turning us in.

Rob: Boy, I have always known where your family was for twenty years. I could have negotiated two hundred million years ago for your whereabouts. I'm fucking loyal! So don't ever ask that question again. Lastly, the main man on that yacht.

Cameron: Yeah, Unc has trusted Rob since day one, you'll.

Andrew: You're right; Jax is sounding like his dad right now, paranoid!

Jax: You funny! So that's the plan then. We are heading to the M. I. A.

Rob: By the where is Paul?

Jax: He is still in pain from his wounds! (Looking at his cousins with his finger over his mouth to keep their mouths shut.)

Rob: Miami it is, but to be on the extremely safe side, I think it best if you guys docked in Fort Lauderdale or the Hollywood area. I want you to stay out of Miami! I'll meet up with you guys around 3 pm.

Carmelo and Jax: Cool!

Rob: I'm jumping on the road with two of my goons from New York. Keep in mind they don't have a clue on what's going on. They are just there for gun power.

We all agreed with Rob on the plans. My cousins and I had two rounds of drinks, and everyone pretty much called it an early night after that. The one thing I'm pretty sure of is that no one got any sleep that night. In the morning, when the captain announced we would be docking within the hour is when shit got real. My damn heart started to race. I started imagining all the forms of outcomes and how this day was going to go. My heart was racing all night, but it was worse now than it already was. My chest felt tight, and it was hard to breathe. I ran to the bathroom and filled the sink with cold water. I just dipped my entire head in the sink three or four times. I had to control my breathing and calm my nerves. My nerves were unstable because all these images and thoughts flooded my mind. In all honesty, I'm sure none of us knew what we were about to get into. Still, we were all in; none of us were turning back because we knew what was at stake. We wanted revenge and blood. In my mind, I wanted everyone to pay dearly. I didn't care if they were the fucking mailman. If anyone liked any of these people, I wanted them dead too. We just didn't have a clue who we were hunting at this point. With all that was on my mind, Ana came walking into my room. She looked confused, lost, puzzled, and scared to death. And had some concerns she wanted to address. We were twenty minutes from docking in Fort Lauderdale.

Ana: Hey, Jax, do you have a quick moment?

Jax: Sure, of course! What's on your mind?

Ana: I'm afraid, to the point where my stomach, heart, and soul feel like they are all going to explode at the same time.

Jax: You're not the only one; I'm sure each one of you is experiencing the same emotions.

Ana: No, Jax, I'm afraid my father is dead as well.

Jax: Cuz, please, please don't think like that. If your father is alive, we are going to find him; I promise you that. I don't even want you thinking negatively right now, either.

Ana: If he was alive, wouldn't we have already heard something from him by now? He would have done anything to let us know he was safe or alive.

Jaylyn: (Walks in) Hey guys, sorry to interrupt, but Rob just called and said he is five minutes away.

Jax: OK, cool! Jaylyn, can you check on Dad? See if the bandages need to be changed. So, we can all go when Rob gets here.

Jaylyn: OK, big bro, I'll take care of him!

Jax: Ana, one moment! (Whispering) just stay close to me, cuz. I'm right here for you!

Shaking her head yes, Ana followed Jaylyn out of the room to prepare for docking in Fort Lauderdale. I threw on some clothes quickly and made my way upstairs to the cockpit to get a bird's eye view of Fort Lauderdale's beaches and unique buildings. I got a totally different feel for Florida than Europe. The air was warm and clear. You could see all the excitement on the beaches two miles from shore. We all dreamed of vacationing in South Florida one day. Just never dreamt in a million years it would be under these circumstances. Carmelo and Andrew also made their way up here to absorb the wonderful view. Moments later, Jaylyn came running in and completely out of breath, screaming, "He isn't in his room; he isn't in his room, and I can't find him."

Jax: Who, Dad?

Jaylyn: Yes, Dad, who else?

Jax: OK, everyone spread out and find him quickly.

Paul: No need. I'm right here. Where are we?

Ana: We're here in Fort Lauderdale, Uncle! Where were you?

Paul: Bathroom! I had to send a fax, or do you need more detail than that?

Jaylyn: Gross Dad!

Paul: OK, and is Rob meeting up with us?

Jaylyn: Yes, he is Dad!

Jax: He is going to meet some guy by the name of La Serpiente. Which is Spanish for…

Paul: The snake, yeah, I know Spanish, son.

Carmelo: (Laughing) Too funny!

Paul: OK, listen up. Safety first, guys. In the large cabinet near my master cabin are a few bulletproof vests. I need each of you to wear one at all times. Keep it when you shit or shower.

Carmelo, Jax, Ana, and Jaylyn: (All at once) Yes, sir!

Paul: Andrew, you and Jax will be coming with me.

Jaylyn: But Dad, you are still pretty hurt and bad.

Paul: (With a dirty look) Jaylyn, Carmelo, and Ana, you guys will stay here on the yacht. Once we step off this yacht, the captain will leave shore and head back to sail. Just a few miles out. I'm leaving anything to chance. Nothing from this point on can go wrong.

Carmelo: Uncle, why aren't we coming with you? We are stronger together as one, right?

Paul: Boy, would you just listen! Ana, can you please upload Andrew's, Jax's and my iPhone into your iPad to start the tracking process for each of us? In case we get split up for any reason. Each of you will text Ana every twenty minutes. Now Ana, if you don't receive a text from each of them every twenty minutes or if their phones go out, Then Jay and Carmelo, you guys rush to the last location that was read on the iPad. So, stay locked, loaded, and ready to roll at the drop of a dime. Kids, if there is any danger, I hate to say this, you shoot every and anything that moves if you feel like your lives are in danger. It's better to ask for God's forgiveness than permission.

Jax: Dad, are you saying you don't trust Rob?

Paul: It's been twenty years, and people have changed. You guys are my only priority. Secondly, I'm pretty sure there's a price on each of our heads now. A few million well and you will be shocked what a man will do for money. I know what I have done.

Andrew, Carmelo, Jax: True, true, true!

Jax: Well, Dad, Rob told us there's a lot on each of our heads and more on yours. But I trust him dad.

Paul: I love Rob, and I do trust him, but I'd rather be sure than sorry. You feel me? Ok, boys, Andrew and Jax take small arms fire with extra clips. 40- or 45-millimeter handguns for some for close-range fire. Pack the Mac-11s with the long suppressors if we are strongly outnumbered.

Andrew: Jax, take two or three handguns each. We got two hands each, bro. If it comes down to I'm unloading 32 instead of 16 in a fool.

Jax: (Laughing) Well your aim ain't never been good!

After our little pow-wow with Pops, we went outside to wait for Rob. Just like a black man to say five minutes when they really meant 15 minutes, which made my father even more cautious and uncomfortable. It was hot and sunny in Fort Lauderdale and tons of beautiful bodies with g-strings walking across the bridge towards the beach area. Andrew and I looked at each other like good God, this was heaven.

Rob finally arrived twenty minutes later in a black Chevy Yukon XL with two of his goons. My father reminded us once again not to trust anyone and to watch each other's back at all costs.

Rob: Paul, oh my God, Paul, it's been too long; give me a hug, bro.

Paul: Easy, easy; I took one in the shoulder and one in the back that came through my stomach a few nights ago.

Rob: What? You shouldn't even be standing up, right? You need any medication or a doctor?

Paul: No, I'll be ok; let's just get this over with.

Rob: Where is everyone else?

Paul: They stay behind!

Rob: Nah, tell them to come along. I want to buy you guys dinner afterward. Catch up, you know!

Paul: Let's just go; the girls are staying put.

This is when I realized my father was brilliant and he knew just what he was doing. When Rob said after the meeting he would get my father's doctor or medication, my father looked at him with an uneasy look. As we sat in the back of the truck, my father was very quiet and paid close attention to where we were going. My father sat right behind Rob with his Glock 40 out on his lap and his finger on the trigger. Rob was sitting up front in the passenger seat and running his mouth nonstop, telling Andrew and me stories about their days in their prime. One of Rob's goons was driving, and the other goon sat behind the driver. That goon seated behind the driver turned to look out the window at some ladies dancing as we drove by. That's when I saw my father quickly drop his cell phone in the back passenger seat pouch. I thought about it: why would he do that? It took me a moment to understand what he was doing. He wanted Ana to track this truck in case something happened to us. He was a fucking genius. We ended up somewhere off Highway 826 by a group of factories in Miami. We could see Miami International Airport from where we were.

Rob: Here we are. It's time to put on your game faces. Remember, these dudes don't play.

Paul: Give me a minute and let me address something with my son really, quick.

Rob: These guys don't like waiting, and we are already five minutes late, man!

Paul: (Angry voice) Rob, I just need a minute with my son. Is that ok?

Rob: (Looking uncomfortable) Ok, Paul, shit!

Paul: Jax, text Ana with this location. Also, have her check all financial records for a Robert. Henry Harris, age 47, of Jacksonville, Florida. Quickly before they notice, son.

Jax: OK, Dad! But why are you checking on Rob's financial records?

Paul: Think If Rob had a wire transfer in the past 24 to 48 hours for a few million dollars. We are dead and that makes one of my oldest friends a fucking rat and you put a bullet in his head before I die today.

Jax: OK, OK, I understand now.

Rob: (Telling from across the parking lot) Paul, what's the holdup? We need to go, bro!

My dad and I exited the truck, and the group of us walked into this large industrial factory and got onto an elevator. It was hard to judge Rob's intention because he kept telling us to stay on point and to watch each other back. The elevator had no button, just a large lever that one of Rob's goon looked at it for a few seconds to figure out how it worked. The right was for up, and the left was for down. With one big push, we headed four flights down. The elevator was extremely slow, and my father asked Rob how business was.

Rob: Business isn't as good as it once was. Those million-dollar days are over with. I have a few strip clubs here in Florida and a couple of car washes. Still, move a few keys here and there to remain a millionaire, you know.

Paul: This is one slow-ass elevator!

Rob: Paul, are you okay? Are you in a hurry? You seem really uneasy and touchy, man.

Paul: We've been through a lot in the last couple of days. So, what do you think?

Rob: Bro, I'm here with you, not against you. I got you!

I didn't want my father to be right about Rob, but I gave Andrew the eye and head nod to watch Rob's goons are really close. I showed him that I had my hand on my Glock and was just waiting for one of them to make a move. The moment the elevator doors open, we were greeted by ten small Mexicans with guns twice their size. They were very hostile and forceful. Pushing and pulling us in the direction they want us to go. They hustled everyone off the elevator and told us to face the wall and get on our knees, hands behind our heads. They search each of us for identification, weapons, and our cell phones. Every word they spoke was in Spanish, no English at all. They had us there for over fifteen minutes, waiting and wondering what they were going to do. Each time Rob would say a word, one of the Mexicans would kick him or slap him with their pistols. He was a pretty hard learner because it took six kicks to his back and four slaps with long riffles into his neck before he started up and shut his mouth.

When Ana didn't get a text from us, we lost our tracking location. She decided to send Carmelo and Jaylyn to our last location. They hustled up and got the Cadillac truck off the yacht. They drove like the devil was on their bumper to get to us. Ana started to worry when she couldn't track Andrew's and Jax's phones anymore. She did not know at the time they were four floors underground. One of the Mexican gunmen took a liking to Paul's cell phone and decided to check it out. Paul's phone started giving out a strong signal, which Ana immediately picked up. She realized that they weren't moving. An overwhelming amount of fear came over Ana. She feared the worst, that everything had gone wrong and everyone was dead.

My father kept whispering to Andrew and me to be brave. Out of nowhere, I heard someone yelling in the dark hallway. It was a female voice saying, "Lavanatie, lavanatie". Then we heard a man's voice standing over us screaming, "Stand up, stand up." So, we did! That same male voice screamed out, "Turn around and keep your hands on your head and follow me." I got a good look at the woman as she walked out from the dark. She was about 5'10 or 5'11, with jet-black flowing hair, high cheekbones, and perfect lips. She was extremely pretty. Her body was exquisite, with mouthwatering hips and ass. Sexy was an understate when looking at her. She had some serious style. Her outfit was all Louis Vuitton, with a skirt and a matching jacket with the L.V. logo imprinted throughout the outfit. Her eyes sparkled like gems when she removed her Chanel sunglasses. She walked ahead of all of us like a boss into a large room with two chairs. They made us stand in a line, shoulder to shoulder, and then we waited for three minutes while she was checking something on her phone. When they felt we were ready, one of the men said something in Spanish, and moments later, a rear door opened. Two tall, muscular Mexican men walked in, followed by the most beautiful woman I had ever seen in my life. She had a silk baby blue Dior fitted pants and a top without sleeves. She was also wearing sunglasses in this dark-ass basement facility. She took a seat next to the other woman who showed something on her phone. One of her Mexican goons brought her a cigarette and then lit it for her. Another goon brought them two tall glasses of champagne. In my mind, I was wondering what the fuck is going on. Why the hell are they playing with us? It was so damn hot down there, but the champagne was overkill. They took their poor time before they acknowledged speaking to us. The lady dressed in Dior and smoking her cigarette introduced herself as the La Serpiente. This pretty much shocked everybody, including Rob, when I heard him say, "Get the fuck out of here."

Rob: Wait, wait, wait a minute, you're the La Serpiente, The Snake?

The Snake: If there is anything wrong with your hearing, then this meeting is going to be longer then I expected it to.

Rob: Nah, my hearing is great, as well as my vision.

The lady dressed in Louis Vuitton nodded at two of their men to remove Rob and his goons. Leaving my father, Andrew, and myself to talk. Rob felt really disrespected when he was shoved out of the room with a gun in his back.

The Snake: What may I do for you, gentlemen? And please be quick about it.

Paul: We need information!

The Snake: Information, do I look like 411 or Google? I don't give out information; information is given to me.

Paul: Is there another name I can address you by? I don't see you as a snake; it does seem lady like.

For some strange reason, this sparked her interest that my father wanted to address her by a more feminine name.

The Snake: What makes you think you will leave alive knowing my name?

Paul: Well, for starters, when your men search for someone, they should ask them to open their hands as well. You never know what someone could hold in the palm of their hand.

Everyone in the room went crazy. Her Mexican gunmen all raised their guns at us while taking four or five steps back. Of all eight of her gunmen, six of them were pointing guns at my father. My heart skipped multiple beats, but the snake seemed cool as a fan. Her men were screaming (put back in the pin) over and over again. The snake's sidekick jumped to her feet like she was ready to run out of her Louis Vuitton skirt. The snake, on the other hand, was as cool as my father was.

Paul: The pin is out, and if we release this clip, we all die in a stinking ass room.

The Snake: You're rather clever! Paul, is it?

Paul: That's my name, yes.

The Snake: It's Erica.

Paul: It's a pleasure, Erica.

Erica: Well, next time, you may want to give me a call. I know some people!

Paul: Yeah, next time! Now, can we get to the business at hand?

Erica: (Smiling) Are you here to talk about protection from the Colombian cartel that is hunting you, your son Jax, your daughter Jaylyn, your niece and two nephews?

Paul: (Looking incredibly puzzled and lost for words)

Jax: What the fuck!

Andrew: (Overly excited and upset) This is fucking unreal. Uncle Paul, it's them. They are the one behind this shit man.

Paul: Andrew, relax and shut up for a moment. How do you know this?

Erica: Like I told you before, information is brought to me. It doesn't matter if it's small or big. I pay top dollar to stay ahead of my competition. You see, you're still alive right now because you are a living legend in this game. The empire you and your family built in the 80s changed the drug game and inspired undesirable men and women like my sister and myself. The stories behind your family flying into the heart of Colombia at a time when bodies were dropping by the minute in the 80's. Just a handful of men were with you, and you took one of your own from the Vasquez brothers without firing a single shot. When the word got out, the Vasquez brothers lost their credibility and became soft. When they couldn't take the pressure that was coming down on them, they killed every man, woman, and child who worked at their estate that day. You also made the Colombian cartels look weak, giving Mexican cartels a strong hold on the import of drugs and the export of cash flow for the Colombian cartels. They tried to show strength by putting out hits on each of your families, hoping to destroy each and every one of you in the worst way possible. A message must be heard worldwide that Colombian cartels were never to be fucked with, the biggest joke after what your families did to them. Instead, one of the Vasquez brothers had his throat cut from ear to ear with his cock still hard, which meant he never got the chance to cum. Another brother died on a casino floor from a deadly poison. The older and wiser of the three brothers was found in a parking lot with a few of his men. Their bodies were all riddled with bullet holes.

Paul: How are you sure it was us? How does anyone know we had anything to do with it?

Erica: Innocent men don't run and hide for twenty years. But because of you and your family taking on the Colombian and putting a major monkey wrench in their operation, it gave birth to Mexican cartels all over Mexico. Because of you, my father, who was born poor, died rich.

Paul: We are really grateful for your history story, but all I want to know is who has a price on my family's head. And where the fuck can I find them.

This whole situation was giving me goosebumps. Hearing about my father and uncles as legends. This had my heart racing and my palms sweating. What was even more confusing was the fact that this beautiful fucking woman was heavily into my old man. When she looked at him, you could see the lust in her eyes for him. She was so turned on while telling us this story. Here I am, 21 years old, six foot three, built like a running back with the sexiest abs you could bounce a quarter off. My damn face belonged on the cover of GQ magazine. The Snake, Ms.

Erica, couldn't stop looking at my father with this look in her eyes that screamed out fuck me raw.

Erica: Millions of dollars are on your and your family's heads, Paul. The Broggest Cartel is responsible for the hit, and from what I know, they have your friend.

Paul: My friend, What friend?

Erica : Huel Hernandez!

Paul: Are you shitting me?

Erica: I'm afraid not!

Jax: How did they get my uncle, and where is he now?

Erica: I was talking to your father, boy!

Jax: Damn the boy talk and damn this bullshit. Where the fuck are they keeping my uncle?

Paul: Jax! Relax, ok, relax!

Erica: I can't say I like your son's attitude! Disrespectful!

Paul: My son's attitude is my problem. Now Huel, where is he, if you know?

Erica: I don't know where they are keeping your friend or how they got him.

Jax: So how the hell do you know any of this is true?

We kind of got the feeling that we crossed the line when she looked at me rather dirty, got up, and walked out without a word. Her goons escorted us back to Rob and his clowns. I could sense that Rob was rather hurt and was in his feelings. For some reason, he couldn't shut his mouth. Rob was asking a million questions. He wanted to know what took place and why wasn't he brought into the sit-down with The Snake. We weren't even out of the custody of Erica's men, and the questions were pouring in, one after the other. Erica's men gave us back our pistols by throwing them on the floor. Each of the guns was given back to us completely empty, with no clips. They followed us to the elevator, watched us close the doors, and headed up. My father didn't pay Rob any attention at all after question after question. We just headed straight for the elevator.

Rob: Paul, I can't help you if I don't know what's going down.

My father took a long look down and noticed Rob's consistent itching of his arms every two to three minutes. Then, my father looked up at me, trying to bring my attention to it by just giving me this look. I looked at Rob but wasn't as quick as my father. I had no idea what he was trying to tell me or what it was I was looking at or for.

Paul: So, Rob, how long has it been since you been on the needle?

Rob: What the hell are you talking about, bro? What needle?

The moment the elevator door opened, my father hustled Andrew and me off. My father looked across the parking lot and noticed two black SUVs facing toward us while a white Rolls Royce was speeding away. At that very moment, my cell phone went off, and a late text message came from Ana. Before I could even think about reading the text, I pulled out my Glock 40 from my waistline. Without anyone noticing, I checked to see if I was fortunate enough to still have one bullet in the chamber. I had a clip hidden in the back of my pants between my belt. Gracefully, I reached for it and loaded my gun. That's when I heard my father say, "We are so fucked." He then briefly pointed at the two SUV's. I wasn't sure what was about to happen at the moment. The look on my father's face and his body language said it all. He was scared to death. My adrenalin instantly started pumping. I felt a warm feeling throughout my body. I could feel the heavy beating of my heart. It was beating harder and faster to the point where you could almost hear your own heartbeat. Everything instantly started to unfold around me in slow motion. Still, it happened so quickly that it was almost hard to keep up. I heard my father's voice scream, "Jax, kill him." My reaction was almost instantaneous. I turned around and dropped to my right knee, and I took aim at Rob's head. I squeezed the trigger, and the sound rang out (Bang). I watched closely, and it was as if I could see the bullet as it ripped through his skin on his forehead. I watched the bullet rip through tissues and bones as his eyes rolled over to the back of his head. His arm flew up into the air wildly, and his tongue hung from his mouth as his body tumbled to the ground. I didn't wait for his body to hit the ground before I aimed for my next target. His goons closest to him were now reaching. He had blood all over his face. I looked in his eye as he tumbled around his holster. I saw the fear in his eyes as he squeezed the trigger. His facial expression said it, and (bang). I opened up his chest, and blood flew everywhere.

This was life, and these actions were all new to me. I knew what was at stake if we failed. Andrew even reacted quickly. While I positioned myself for the second goon, Andrew was already wrestling him to the floor. My father was quick to help Andrew. The two of them had him on his back in seconds as I rushed over. Andrew was on the ground choking him, giving me a clear shot. I didn't want to waste a single shot. The look in his eyes said, please don't. He was afraid. It didn't matter cause I wasn't going to let my father down. Everyone in my mind had to go that killed my mother and my family. A rage exploded in me and (bang, bang). I put two large holes in his chest. My father was holding his wounds where he had been shot. I heard Andrew's voice, "The trucks." We all heard a vehicle racing towards us. I turned to see that two black SUVs were actually ours. The trucks came barrel through the ten-foot gates and hit two cars as well. The trucks came to a screeching sideways stop. Just inches from us, Jaylyn and Carmelo jumped out of the trucks. They were both wearing bulletproof vests and full tactical gear. Jaylyn was holding an M4 machine gun, which might have weighed more than her. Carmelo said, "Who is he? It was one of The Snakes, aka Erica men. He was flat face down with his hands over his head. Shaking and damn near crying. Carmelo and Andrew grabbed him and stood him up. When he heard my father say, "Don't kill him." The guy pissed on himself.

My pops just laughed when he saw this stone-cold Mexican cartel killer relieve himself when he thought he was about to die. He wasn't exactly safe yet. We were about to squeeze him for information. As Carmelo and Andrew gagged him, tied him, and tossed him in the back of the truck. My father pulled me aside to ask me the craziest question ever.

Paul: Jax, why the hell did you shoot Rob?

Jax: What are you serious?

Paul: Yes, I'm serious!

Jax: Dad, you told me to shoot him.

Paul: I was talking about Erica's man. The one who pissed on himself.

Jax: Dad, your friend had a wire transfer of three million transferred into his personal account in the last 24 hours. Ask Ana to confirm it because I have the text from her right here, Dad.

Paul: He was one of my closest friends, Jax. Next time, check with me before you take it upon yourself to do something crazy like that.

Jax: What? What just happened here? I'm supposed to check with you. Who sent you a memo? Are you shitting me, right?

My father had the weirdest way of saying he was proud when we did something amazing. Unfortunately, this wasn't one of those moments. He was hurt! Rob was one of his closest friends and business associates from his childhood. I had to swallow my pride and hold back my words. Everything around us was shit and we kept inheriting more and more shit.

The next question on the agenda was about that speeding white Rolls Royce. When we asked Carmelo and Jaylyn about it; they had no clue who was in that Rolls Royce. They told my dad that they both almost crashed into Rolls, rushing to our aid. My father was overwhelmed with questions he wanted answers too. We took Erica's guy with us on the yacht. We pounded him the whole ride back to the yacht. We tied his ass up and gagged him. He kept telling us he wouldn't say shit and we could kiss and lick certain parts of his body. I would rather just shoot off with a twelve-gage shotgun.

Carmelo: Yo, Unc, I thought the plan was we were going to make him talk and tell us something, anything about the situation we are in.

Paul: Once we get going, he will not only talk but also sing.

Jaylyn: Where are we going?

Paul: It's a little surprise and class is in session kids.

Chapter Eight
Men Overboard

We got back to the yacht and smuggled this guy onto the yacht without anyone seeing us, especially anyone from the crew. Ana got the captain to sail for about two hours out to sea. That's when we saw a different side of my father. My pops were calm as we watched this hundred-and-sixty-pound man freeze from a camera inside the freezer. He seemed absolutely heartless to me. Under these circumstances, I fully understood how my father was feeling. He stood there with his hands crossed over his chest, explaining, "This man would be dead in an hour. So, we'll let him freeze for 45 minutes. If he doesn't talk by then, we make it worse by throwing hot water on his cold body and sticking him back in the freezer for 30 minutes. Once he can't feel any of his private body parts and the pain becomes too much, he'll sing before his body shuts down, and then we'll throw his body overboard." And just like that, he walked away.

The 45 minutes were up, and my father gave us the ok to take him out of the freezer. My heart went out to this guy. He cried, begging us to kill him. He screamed out in Spanish, "Just please don't put me back in there." My father told him in Spanish he had a warm blanket and fireplace for him to get warm if he told us who Erica was. Who was she working for? Who was behind the hit of our family? During those two hours in the kitchen, walking in the deep freezer, he still refused to talk. He told my father in Spanish to kill him, fuck it 'cause she would kill his whole family.

My father told him killing him was too easy. He has yet to feel pain. We stuck him back in the freezer. He screamed and yelled out of anger. He was a strong little dude. When the cold water hit his body, the freezer door closed. I watched this man cry in pain and agony. My father gave two shits on what he was putting this man through. The first five minutes shake from the brutal cold. Ten minutes into, he was so cold he couldn't shake anymore. His skin color was almost white as chalk. His eyes were closed as if he were dead. Fifteen minutes later, my father told us to remove him. He gave us the ok to wrap him in a blanket. I could see that Ana didn't approve of my father's actions. So, she bought him three buckets, hoping it would warm him up quickly. My father asked us all to leave the room and close the door behind us. So, we all did with the unknowing feeling of what he was about to do to this man.

Twenty minutes passed before the door reopened, and my father walked out. I was the first to ask him if the guy talked. My father didn't answer. He just looked more upset than he was before. He called out, "Carmelo, Jax," and we walked over to him. He told us he was giving him an hour or so to warm up, and he would take it from there. He asked us to go to the freezer and get thirty pounds of beef and warm it up. He wanted to make sure the beef had lots of warm blood in it. Carmelo and I looked at each other, completely confused, but we did just what he asked us to do.

Roughly two hours had gone by, and Erica's Goon was pretty much warmed up. He was still shaking, and the fear was written all over his face. At this point, my father hadn't said a single word to any of us about what had happened in that room with Erica's goon. My father gave us an order to get him and bring him to the back of the yacht. The minute we grabbed him, he started screaming and begging us, "No, no, no." He just kept screaming, "No, no, no." When

Carmelo and I got him to the back of the yacht, my father took a moment and looked at this guy with such disgust.

Paul: Carmelo, you and Jax strip this fool completely naked.

Jax: What?

Carmelo: Naked? You mean you want us to take another man's clothes off?

Jax: You serious? Why?

The look my father gave us, we didn't ask another question. We just did what he asked of us. Once he was naked, my father walked around him twice with a very large knife in his hand. Ana was holding a bucket filled with bloody beef. Carmelo and I just took it as a way of scaring Erica's goon shitless. It was kind of funny to all of us looking at this man naked. His dick shriveled up into his balls. His head was up and back like he was praying to God. He stood there naked, shaking and crying. Father said, "Jax, tie this rope around his feet." I wondered why if his

hand was cuffed behind his back. I didn't ask any questions; I just followed his orders. I tied this thick rope around his feet and then looked into his eyes. He was begging me without a word not to do whatever was about to take place. My father told Carmelo and Andrew to hold him tight.

Paul: Your last opportunity to talk.

Guy: Fuck you, 'cause you're all dead. Your all fucking dead, puta.

Paul: You know who I am, right? Do you know what this puta is capable of? I'm made motherfuckers like you, my punk bitches all my life. I have served a thousand of you pretends. Wet behind the ears can't piss straight little pussies.

Andrew: Wait, did this bastard speak English the whole time?

Carmelo: That shit just blows me. Lying ass dude.

Jax: Will you two shut the hell up?

Paul: Tell me what the hell I want to know.

Guy: Just kill me already, puta.

My father smiled at Erica's goon. Then, his smile turned into an evil frown. He was either frustrated or straight up and down, losing his mind about what he would do next. I watched my father cut this man twenty-two times. His leg, his arms, stomach, neck, face, back, even on his ass cheek. Blood was slowly pouring down every inch of his body. It didn't take long till he was covered completely in blood. This goon dropped to his knees but still refused to talk. Either this Erica was the real deal, or this man was beyond loyal to her. My father then grabbed the bucket with bloody beef parts and poured them overboard. He then turned to Erica's goon and told him. We are in the most shark-infested waters in South Florida. We all looked overboard, and he was right. There were sharks heading towards us at high speeds as far as our eyes could see. There were sharks coming from every direction. Those sharks were drawn to that blood-like crack to a crackhead. I counted seven fins in the water. My father grabbed Erica's goon by the back of his neck and bent him over the railing with brute force. My father wanted him to view the sharks for himself. He took a deep breath and closed his eyes. He simply started to cry again, real tears. I could tell he had already accepted his fate. My father asked him one last time, "Are you going to tell me what I want to hear?" He just shook his no and said, "They would wipe out my whole family." I fully understood his logic and committed to his family. Cause we had that same commitment.

My father looked at Carmelo, Andrew, and me, and we knew we were throwing this man overboard to his death. We each grabbed a firm hold of his bloody body. We lifted him straight in the air as he kicked and screamed out no., I closed my eyes when we let him go. I heard his body hit the water almost instantly. I didn't want to see it. I could hear his bones being bitten into as he broke from the shark's powerful jaw. His screams didn't last very long. I could hear my cousin's voice yell, "God damn, holy shit." It was a hard situation to digest. When I opened it, I looked into the cold, dark water. It was flooded with blood and guts. Ana and Jaylyn were vomiting up their guts from the vicious, brutal sight of what they had just witnessed.

I turned to my father to see his reaction to the action he had just made us part take, but he was gone. I had no idea if he stuck around after we picked him in the air. Carmelo and Andrew was laughing. Two of them were playing tough and laughing at girls for vomiting on themselves. I was too with the thought of who my father really was. He had shown me a side that I had never seen before. He was heartless, violent, and ruthless to the core. I know we lost my mother, my cousin, and people we all loved dearly, but I was consumed with the thought that I'd never get back the father I really knew.

I knew we weren't going to see my father for the rest of the night, but I needed some solid, real answers from him. I needed to know what we were becoming. I felt like a monster, a heartless killer who would go to any level for vengeance. The consistent question in my head was, what were we becoming with each lethal action we were taking? I needed answers cause for me I wanted to know when this would be over. What kind of life were we going to have after this? So, I gathered up my stomach to march right into my father's room in search of those answers. What I found was even more disturbing. I found my father curled in a dark corner of his room. He was holding something firmly against his chest. His knees were curled up to his chest as he cried. My father was holding a picture of my mother. I witnessed firsthand his heartbreak. I witnessed how badly this whole ordeal was affecting my father. He was at his breaking point. I realized that moment that my questions we're going to have to wait. Instead, I just wanted to be there for the only parent I had left. So, I propped myself on the floor next to my father and just cuddled up next to him, and I held him close. He cried for two hours straight, at least, until we both fell asleep in that corner. The next morning, there was a strong, assertive knock on his door, which made both of us jump out of our sleep. We looked at each other like we were both misplaced by someone else. My father asked me to get the door, and it was the captain. The casita was breathing rather heavily. He was out of breath, which only meant he ran to my father's room with something urgent to say. The captain looked past me and straight to my father. Neither one of them said a word; they just looked with signals. So, my father invited the captain into his room. The captain quickly walked over to him and whispered something confidential in his ear. My father looked seriously surprised and shocked at the same time. His only words were, "Are you shitting me," and the captain just shook his head with serious confirmation. The captain and my father hurried out of the room, and I followed blindly behind them.

Our breath was hot and cold in our eyes; we headed up to the stern of the yacht. At a really close distance, I could hear a helicopter approaching. We were in open waters, I'm sure, cause that's what my father instructed the captain to do each night for our safety. My father looked back at me before walking out on the deck and placing both hands on my shoulders. He looked concerned into my eyes and asked me to wait there. I heard the helicopter was right above us. I asked him why, and he answered, "For your safety, son". He then turned and walked away from me. One of his bodyguards closed the door behind him after my father walked out to greet whoever was about to land. I needed to see for myself, so I ran to the starboard side of the yacht to get a better look. I didn't want to be seen and have my father mad cause I didn't listen to his instructions. I just cracked the door and looked out, hoping that no one saw me. I witnessed the captain and three of the yacht's security guards waiting with guns. They were aiming and waiting patiently for whoever was about to exit the helicopter. I watched from a distance as the helicopter landed and doors opened. Our security was screaming, showing us your hands over and over again as the people on the helicopter slowly exited the craft. To my damn surprise, it was Erica and second in command. The sexy lady was with her during our last encounter. The both of them still dress to kill. They were both wearing white fitted see-through suits with pants. They were pretty much matching this time, down to their matching YSL black heels but carrying different color Hermès bags. Erica's bag was green, and her second bag was yellow.

This was the moment I knew the tides had changed in our favor. I knew the ball was in our court this time around. After Erica and her second exited the helicopter, two of her men did the same. The two men were rushed to the floor, facing down with knees on their backs. The captain searched the two men and found two Heckler & Koch SP5 small fire machine guns on them. The captain searched the ladies last, and inside those expensive Hermès bags were two Heckler & Koch P30SK
9mm handguns. All I could think to myself was that these people really knew their guns. As security quickly disarmed them of their weapons and walked them into the lounge area of the yacht. I looked past the helicopter to see Ana and Jaylyn run up to the port side of the yacht. Just on the opposite side, I also witnessed what was taking place. Carmelo and Andrew came up behind me with twenty-one questions. We all just stood on the steps and watched as my father and security escorted them away.

My father didn't treat them the way they treated us on our first meeting. He had food and drinks brought to them. Their security was brought to our media and game room while the ladies held a meeting with my father. A good twenty minutes had gone by before my father sent one of his security guards to come and get each one of us. I'm pretty sure we were all nervous and anxious to know what was going on.

From the moment we entered the room, Erica sat in front of my father with tears in her eyes. I was a bit lost on what was taking place and eager to find out what was taking place. She seemed scared, and her friend or second was rubbing her back to console her. My father took the time to introduce each of us to Erica and her best friend slash conciliatory, Bianca McKnight. The two ladies gave us a brief history of their friendship. There were a few attempts on Erica's family's lives from the time she was three years old till her eighth birthday. Erica's father was concerned for his daughter and mother's safety. So, at the age of eight, Erica's father put her and her mother on a plane to Europe. Erica's mother wasn't Colombian but rather Russian Irish. So, Erica's father sent them away to live in Paces, Europe, for a few years. That is where she met her best friend Bianca, who is of Irish descent. Bianca's family had passed away in an Irish mob bombing of her family home in Ireland. Bianca was only twelve years old at the time. Not a single person in her extended family wanted to take her in because of the. Fear of having their families or themselves massacred. Erica begged her mother to do the right thing and take in Bianca. So, they legally adopted Bianca, making them sisters.

The two young ladies grow up together in a happy, caring, and loving environment. Until Erica's mother went to visit their father in Medellin, Colombia, for a month. A trip the girls passed up to go skiing with friends in Switzerland. The girls were just barely twenty-one at the time. Erica's mother was leaving Colombia to return to Europe when her three-car convoy was ambushed. Everyone who was with her was massacred. Erica's mother's severed head was delivered to her father the same day. Her father suffered a stroke and heart attack the moment he saw his wife's head without her body. At that moment, I could fully understand why my father would consider being so hospitable to them. My heart was hurting for them because we were suffering from the same situation.

Erica continued to tell us her uncle took over leadership of her father's cartel, which at this point was rather weak. Their cartel was considered a joke to most in Colombia, and their partners in Mexico. There were new drug cartels and crews every year that were taking over her father's territories for some years. Erica explained that her father was barely holding on to the drug game anymore. He was able to find ten or so other financial income streams outside of the cocaine and heroin business. Businesses that were also making the family very wealthy. Erica's father wanted out of the drug game and was preparing to leave Colombia and cocaine to be a legitimate businessman in Europe. Erica explained that once her uncle took leadership, it was in hopes that she would step up and take her father's place. Her hands were forced when her uncle was murdered three months after her father's stroke and heart attack. Her uncle was found dead in his home with three bullet holes in his chest and one in his head while sitting on the toilet. Her father was still alive, but his brain was pretty much a vegetable and still is. She refused to pull the plug on the machines, keeping him alive at this point. For the past three years, she's been using her father's cartel to find her mother and uncle's killers. She explained how disgusted she is with what she has become, but she can't look back now. She ordered the deaths of so many people that she knows her soul will burn in hell forever. She won't stop until everyone involved has paid with their lives.

My father asked her why she put a hit on all of us in the nicest way he could. Erica answered by saying she didn't order any hits on us. She explained she had cars posted three blocks away on six different streets. The same streets all lead to the location where we were meeting. I laughed and asked her what kind of school she attended to be so strategic. Bianca answered,

"The Royal Military Academy in the United Kingdom." It was safe to say everyone in the room was speechless at her answer to my question. Bianca explained that they ran just like we did when they were told these SUVs were coming. She also explained that there were four SUV's. Two others followed them for ten miles, riddling their Rolls Royce with bullet holes. Luckily, their car was armor-proof with bulletproof windows. The conversation with the ladies went on for two hours straight.

My father was an incredibly smart man, and life has taught him to always be ten steps ahead of everyone else. He whispered something to the captain before asking everyone else to leave the room beside Erica and Bianca. The moment we exited the room, the captain had us gathered around him. The captain's message from my father was for all of us to stay alert and have weapons on us at all times. The message was simple and straightforward. My father for sure didn't know how Erica and her people had found us in open water. I knew the situation was serious when I saw our three-hundred-pound chief had a shotgun in hand ten minutes later. For the next two hours straight, every man and woman working this yacht was checking the seas, air, and the ship for possible threats. Nothing or no one was found, of course, but it was better to be safe than seriously sorry. The captain was hard at work looking into the lady's story to see if what they said matched up. It was a blessing to have a real British naval officer as your captain. He had connections with the CIA and British intelligence. He could tell anyone and anyone's secrets by the end of the day.

Chapter Nine
Drastic Measures

When I couldn't take it anymore, my curiosity got the best of me. I wondered if my father had told
the ladies how he had fed their man to some hungry sharks the day before. I needed to know the real reason why they were on our yacht. I walked into the main dining room, where the ladies were relaxing as if they were on vacation. The ladies had their shoes off and their bare feet on our sofas. While enjoying one of the four bottles of Domaine de la Romanee-Conti, we had on board the yacht.

Jax: I see you ladies are enjoying yourselves. Drinking a 17,000.00-euro bottle of wine.

Bianca: I'm pretty sure it's pennies from where I'm sitting.

Erica: Bee, be nice, please.

Jax: What is it that you want? Better yet, why are you really here?

Erica: We help you, and you help us.

Jax: With what?

Bianca: It's very simple. Your father has agreed to work with us. You'll help find the people who are hunting down your family. In turn, you will help with our opposition.

Jax: (Laugh) So you want to team up with us?

Erica: You can call it that, Jaxon. In military school, they teach you straight in numbers.

Jax: Sounds really great; thanks for the lesson.

Bianca: You're welcome!

Jax: Let me ask you this: how do we know we can trust you?

Erica: Honestly, you don't, Jax. But here is the reality of the situation. We are both outgunned and outnumbered apart. We personally have no issues with your family. We couldn't give two shits about this drug game or the so-called empire my father built. Because of this business, countless amounts of family and friends are six feet deep.

Bianca: I asked your father about that point. From the stories we have heard, he knows all too well.

Jax: Or maybe you're playing the sympathy role because you know the stories.

Erica: Google me! Erica Marie Santana.

Jax: I have, and your stories match up, every word. You told us your father was dead when we first met you.

Bianca: He's a vegetable. To some of us, he is dead. To Erica, he isn't. That man is all she has to hold on, too, Jax.

Jax: Well, in that case, my condolences. I'm sorry if I was out of place.

Erica had tears in her eyes again. I can see this was a super touchy subject for her, and Bianca was like her bodyguard and protector. I spent another twenty minutes with the ladies, getting to know them and seeing where their heads were at. Once you're able to peel away some of those guarded layers, I found them to be rather intriguing and playful. I'm sure their playful side was all the wine they were indulging in at our expense. Mainly cause those wines belonged to my mother. She wanted to save a bottle for each of our wedding days to come. A plan she had that she is no longer here to see come through.

My father walked in a few minutes later to witness the buffoonery that was taking place. Erica was so drunk had fallen off the sofa three times in two minutes. She and Bianca finished three bottles of wine and a full bottle of Don Julio 1942. My father had security, and two female yacht attendees help them to a suite on the upper deck of the yacht, not far from my father's suite. Our security had to stand guard by their room all night and witness their whereabouts at all times. Not to mention the twenty-two cameras on that floor. Their two bodyguards were also watched closely all night as well. I must say it was a relief to wake up and be told by security that they were well-behaved. They didn't try anything at all. The next morning, my father had a large feast prepared for breakfast. I'm guessing in honor of the ladies and our new partnership with them. I'm talking eggs, scrambled, over easy, and three different kinds of omelets. There were Benedicts, bacon, foot-long sausages, waffles, pancakes, French toast, fruit, orange juice, coffee, and the list goes on. The two ladies who came to join us just wore robes and sunglasses. Andrew and Carmelo's hormones were through the roof when they saw Erica and Bianca in their robes. The ladies looked to be suffering from a serious hangover. Bianca sat down and inhaled the food and immediately jumped back, ran to the railing, and started to vomit overboard. My family and I started to laugh. Erica simply turned around, looking at Bianca's vomit while sipping a large cup of coffee. The two ladies were too hungover to even eat. I'm sure the crew and security didn't mind all that food.

The ladies didn't stay at breakfast long at all. They drank a cup or so of black coffee and returned to their room to clean up. We didn't see Erica and Bianca again for about two hours. When they came out of their room, it was like a runway show with dark Chanel sunglasses over their eyes. Both ladies were wearing their hair down, and their outfits hugged them like elastic. They were dripped in Harry Winston and Cartier diamonds. Both the ladies were wearing Chanel from head to toe. Erica had on a Cartier Santos XL Skeleton watch encrusted with full cuts of emerald diamond throughout the entire watch. Bianca had the same watch on, but Her's had VVS round stones. On the other hand, the ladies had white, yellow, and rose gold Cartier bracelets flooded with diamonds. Around their necks, they both were wearing matching white diamond chains with a huge thirteen-carat Harry Winston heart-shaped yellow canary diamond to match their yellow Chanel pumps. Even the two fashionistas, Ana and Jaylyn, were extremely impressed by their style. Carmelo and Andrew both just wanted to rip their clothes off of them. They were everything a man could dream of.

My father called for afternoon tea and a sit down with the ladies to see how we could help each other. What Erica did next stopped my father in his tracks and amazed each of us. For me, it brought on a whole other extreme sexiness about her. Erica pulled out a weed grinder, her marijuana and rolled a joint. He took three strong pulls and put her head to enjoy the hit from the marijuana, slowly releasing smoke from her nose before hitting it again three times and passing it to Bianca. No one said a word because it was so unexpected. When I looked around the room Ana, Jaylyn, Carmelo, and Andrew were smiling. My father wasn't smiling but his mouth was open wide in disbelief. The ladies did offer, and everyone politely refused, but Carmelo. He was about to reach for the blunt and caught himself when he saw the look my father gave him.

After that amazing moment, we got down to business. The ladies enlightened us with some very valuable intel. It seemed that men my father and uncles took out over twenty years ago had offspring as well. One of Vasquez's brothers had a daughter, Mila, and a son, Andres. They were now running their own operation with the help of their mother, Yinnsely. They weren't established as a cartel or had any cartel connections. Their operation was run like a real LLC with even a brand name for their cocaine. They were the growers and producers. Their business partner was the distributor. They ran a minimum-risk operation with the protection of a Colombian military colonel. This colonel was their business partner and had control of three thousand men and women who would gladly kill for him. It was a 50/50 deal and Colonel Narciso Rodriguez gave Vasquez a guarantee that any product lost on his end would come out of his pocket.

The mother, Yinnsely, promised her kids she would find and bury the men responsible for their father's death. She swore to her kids she would annihilate their entire families if it was the last thing she did on this earth. Bianca went further by saying she had spent millions over the years looking for Ernesto and his brother. She knew if she found them, she would also find you and your family, Paul.

Paul: What's your angle in all of this? Did they have something to do with your family's murder? Why are you giving us this information?

Bianca: Paul, again, try to understand for the past six- or seven years, Erica's father has been doing everything in his power to escape the cartel and everyone involved with that life.

Erica: My father built five eighty-million-dollar luxury apartment buildings all over Western Europe so that none of us would ever have to look over our shoulder again.

Jax: We get that!

Erica: Let me finish, Jax, and you'll get a full understanding of why we are here with you. The Santana family once worked for the Vasquez brothers and the Medellin Cartel. When the Medellin Cartel turned to shit and bodies started dropping everywhere. Friends started turning on friends. Brother setting up brothers for the sole purpose of self-preservation. My family got the opportunity we deserved to branch out on their own and become our own cartel and my father and mother funded it all themselves. We had seven hundred acres in Monteria, where we grow our own coca leaves. I processed it there, and then it was an easy boat ride over to Panama City. It was so close we could do three trips in one day. It was as if we became millionaires overnight. As a child, all I could remember before moving to Europe was that the homes kept getting bigger and bigger every year. Yinnsely didn't see my father's success as her own. In her eyes, she gave it to use. When she turned to my father in her time of need and my mother told him to stay out of her cartel war, she used every resource she had to destroy my family.

Bianca: We can't prove it, but we know she is responsible for Erica's mother's death. Erica's uncle, who had been a California lawyer for ten years, came to work for her father. He wasn't built for this kind of lifestyle. He cooked the books and handled the legitimate side of the family business. When he was forced to step up as boss, the first thing he did was take a meeting with Yinnsely and her kids. Less than five minutes from her home, his car was shot up.

Erica: Her daughter Mila called me right after, in Europe, to tell me I'm next.

Bianca: Two days after that, we had lawyers telling us Erica is now head of her father's cartel and CEO of all his legal business ventures.

Erica: The following day after that, I had someone try and kill me at a spa.

Bianca: We've been pretty much on the run and trying our best to stay two steps ahead of the Vasquez family by paying any price for valuable intel on them and whoever surrounds them and their madness.

Paul: I have one question. How did you acquire the name the Snake?

Erica: (Laughing) Well, I reached out to Ms. Yinnsely personally to see if we could resolve whatever situation she may have with my family. On the phone, she kept calling me a snake and referring to my family as snakes. We stole our position from her family like a snake. So, I told her if she sends anyone else after us, I promise her she won't see this snake coming.

Ana: Well, did she send anyone after you after that?

Bianca: Yes, she did one after the other.

Carmelo: So, how did you deal with it?

Erica: We buried everyone she sent after us. We are no fools. We hired real mercenaries to work for us.

Jaylyn: I don't think I've ever heard of Mexican mercenaries, ever.

Bianca: We have a Mexican associate who is highly invested in our survival. He sent us thirty of his best guns for hire.

Paul: Just so you know, we took one of your men when we left the warehouse, barely with our lives.

Bianca: Well, where is he?

Paul: Well, he wouldn't talk, so I fed him to the sharks.

Bianca: Oh my God, are you serious?

Jax: Is that going to be a problem with our new arrangement?

Erica: These men knew what they signed up for.

Bianca: I guess thank you for your honesty. We will have to reach out to our friend in Mexico to ensure his family is taken care of.

Paul: Words are words! How do I know what you're saying is absolutely accurate?

With that question, the ladies brought out all forms of receipts to back up their story. The biggest shocker was a full HD video recording of Ms. Yinnsely Vasquez's bounty on each of our heads. After the recording, we were all speechless at that point. There were so many questions on the table but the most important was how do we deal with Yinnsely and her kids.

Erica and Bianca were still two very young women. Despite the unfortunate circumstances they were forced into, they both love to party and have a good time. From my brief observation, they really didn't care who else was there. As long as they were together, they would have ensured each other had a great time. They encouraged us to let loose, kick off our shoes, and enjoy the night. Bianca went down to the wine cellar, and the cooler brought some more expensive wine along with five bottles of Crystal and five bottles of Ace of Spades. They didn't ask permission to do anything. You could see their lifestyle was spoiled rich girls who got whatever they wanted. So, Ana and Jaylyn got along with them really well.

Andrew and Carmelo enjoyed partying with them as well. My father, the captain and I sat close by most of the night as we watched them all dance the night away. My mind was more concerned with all that was going on in our world. I picked up on my father's concern for me. That's when he said, "Son, go and join them; stop stressing yourself." "Son, the way things are right now tomorrow isn't promised to any of us." I knew I was my father's backbone now. I also knew how everything was affecting him in the worst way. I had to ask him twice to make sure he wanted me to leave his side. He just gave me a reassuring smile, looked at me, and said, "Captain Von and I are old men. We'll live vicariously through you, Jax." My father's smile just meant the world to me at that moment. So, I turned and walked down to the lower pool deck to join the party. Erica seemed happier than everyone else, so I decided to let loose and party with them. She ran straight towards me with open arms and embraced me with both arms around my neck. She kept a strong grasp on her champagne bottle, which was still in hand. She looked me straight in the eyes and bit her bottom lips with a seductive smile. Her body language and stare said she wanted me. I have to say I liked it a lot. I felt warm inside almost immediately, so I wrapped my hands around her hips, with my hand slightly on her butt, just enough for her to notice. She quickly blushed and pulled herself even closer to me. We danced, we laughed and even cuddled while we danced without ever saying a word to each other all night. Erica had all her focus on me and nothing else. She slowly tilted my head back and poured champagne into my mouth over and over again. For the next few hours, we all just let loose. Once Andrew and Carmelo had two bottles of champagne in their system, they started taking off their clothes, one piece at a time, till they were both in their boxers and diving into the dark black ocean. The girls loved it. They all screamed and cheered those two knuckleheads on.

The next morning, I woke up with loud sounds of helicopter engines and rotors. The headache was instantaneous. I was mad at the sudden noise and the disrespect anyone would start a helicopter this early in the morning. I could barely remember anything after the second bottle of champagne. All I know is I woke next to Erica and the rear deck of the yacht. The hot sun was beaming directly down on us, so it wasn't early. My neck and back felt like bacon being cooked.

What burnt more was noticing Erica, and I were both fully dressed. I knew then that nothing sexual had taken place between us last night. Bianca seemed to have already been up for a few hours. She had showered, did her hair differently from last night, and had on something sexy for the day. A black two-piece bikini. She was smiling at Erica and me with a little smart remark. She said, "Didn't want to wake the love birds too early. You both looked so peaceful together." I honestly didn't know if I should blush or play tough. Erica quickly changed the subject by asking Bianca if their men were leaving already. Bianca smiled at her and answered, "Yes, girl, it's noon already." I instantly had concerns and asked why they had left. Erica answered, "To get the men still loyal to me ready for this war." I knew in my heart I really liked Erica, but I didn't trust her, nor Bianca. I had this gut feeling that they weren't telling us everything. I knew in my heart they had a hidden agenda, and so did my father. I knew he was just playing along for the long game.

Chapter Ten
Revenge Is the Best Dish

Erica and Bianca expressed some ideas they were brainstorming. It seems the Vasquez family took over her father's export ideas after successfully sabotaging his business for some years. The Vasquez's family had taken a lot of different angles in making sure Erica's father lost four to five of every cargo of cocaine he shipped from Colombia to Panama City. They used the police or military to seize the cargo. They have subcontracted Costa Rican, Jamaican, and Haitian pirates to steal the cargo, murder her father's entire crew so no one would be willing to work for him out of fear of never returning back home. They paid out millions to the pirates so they could bring the cargo to Vasquez's front door. Where they turned around and made a huge profit from her father's cocaine. Erica said that the most effective and cheapest the Vasquez would use was bombing her father's ships. Erica's father was losing millions a day, and this was crippling his business. The worst part of the situation was that Erica's father didn't have the manpower, and Vasquez had to go to war with them. If he even attempted that, he knew he would lose everything. It didn't matter how many times they forced his hand. The Vasquez's always seemed to have the upper hand.

Erica's father decided to take a bigger risk by shipping his cargo straight up the coastline to Nicaragua, as the area they were in was notorious for thieves who might seize the cargo and even murder his men. Worst yet, lose the shipment along with his men and his ship. It got to the point where a lot of the Mexican cartels wouldn't do business with him because the cargo kept getting lost. Erica's father had to sell his load for a fraction of the loss. He was making pennies on the dollar.

The ladies explained things got even worse when her father's best friend got involved. He contacted a small group of American mercenaries to find the rat inside her father's Organization who was feeding the Vasquez valuable information on their loads and daily operations. They were also paid to kill anyone who was associated with the Vasquez's organization. It was a campaign that went on for three years. The mercenaries were very effective with the security of transportation of their loads up the coastline to Nicaragua. They would escort the shipment with four military-type boats that were armed with fifty-caliber machine guns. Different types of rocket launches and underwater missiles. Pirates ships never saw those missiles until they were burning in a hell storm of fire. Erica's father went from taking losses to a profit margarine, which was unbelievable.

The mercenaries were so effective that they planted listening devices throughout Erica's family homes and cars. It took them many months before they found a husband and wife who worked for her family. This husband and wife were selling inside secrets to the Vasquez family. The husband was a groundskeeper, and the wife was a maid and prep cook for Erica's family. Any and everything they heard in the house that was valuable information they sold to Vasquez's family for thousands of dollars. They were caught more than once discussing private information among themselves, which wasn't enough to mark them as rats until a dead giveaway. The husband was caught saying, "They are going to pay us big for this information," to his wife, who co-signed, saying, "This is making us so rich." Erica's father was informed immediately by his hired guns, and ten minutes later, the husband and wife found themselves tied up and beaten.

Erica said the husband and wife were brutally tortured as their children and grandparents watched. Their children cried and begged for their parents' lives. The lead mercenary went by the name Alpha and Alpha convinced Erica's father to allow them to hand out the most violent punishment. A punishment so harsh no one would dare cross him or his family like this again. Erica stated her father wasn't a violent man by nature, but he quickly agreed with Alpha. Alpha had his men massacre the children and grandparents in front of the mother and father but decapitated both parents. The parents' heads were sent to the Vasquez main residents.
This indicated that her family had found Vasquez's rat. Without inside information, Vasquez took to the violent streets. More blood was being spilled, and neither side was making any money. The smaller organizations were feeding their pockets from this war and becoming cartels themselves. Erica's father lost full control when her mother was murdered and left Colombia. Eight of the twelve mercenaries were killed that day as well. The last four packed up and left Colombia in the middle of the night.

Erica and Bianca's story was explosive. It left all of us pretty much speechless. Erica asked us if we remembered when she told us she paid for good information. My father and I answered yes. She explained something she learned from her father and Vasquez's war between the two. The Vazquez always had the upper hand because they had valuable information on her family's business. She explained with a devilish grin that she had spent the last year getting five people inside the Vasquez family impound. An impound that was fortified and rebuilt since Paul, my father, and uncles walked in there and took Uncle Ernesto out without killing anyone. Erica said, "It's time to turn the tables on them and destroy their business and family with it." My father's smile was unbelievable.

My father sat back on the deck, watching the beautiful blue ocean with his Tom Ford sunglasses and smoking one of his very expensive Gurkha Black Dragon Cigar. He was in the best mood I have seen him in days. He was calm and relaxed as if he knew today was going to be a great day for him. He nonchalantly pulled out his phone and texted the captain to head toward the war zone, Colombia. Erica said her men were going to meet us in Cartagena, Colombia. She had a simple and straightforward plan after the Vasquez family took over her family's shipping ports in Puerto Escondido and Los Cordobas. The ports now served as the Vasquez's import and export hub for their cocaine distribution business. They had a fleet of ships and boats docked there. We were going to do what they did to Erica's family. Send entire shipments and ships to the bottom of the ocean. Erica had intel from her spies inside the Vasquez's organization. Their main cocaine plant produced just over half a billion dollars in cocaine per month. The plant was located in the countryside of San Pedro, just north of Medellin. We knew that in two days, four ships were leaving Colombia with the estimated value of a hundred million dollars of cocaine. One ship was going to the ocean borders of Puerto Rico and the Dominican Republic. Two ships just north to Belize City in Belize for three different Mexican cartels. The last one was to the Cayman Islands for its final destination, Miami, Florida.

We were going to conduct a simultaneous attack on the ships and the cocaine plant. An attack that would cost the Vasques a cool billion dollars. We weren't just sinking their transport ships and boats. We were also sinking the family's prize possession. A one hundred million dollar mega yacht they had just recently purchased from a tech billionaire. It also seemed that Alpha, the mercenary that had recently worked for Erica's father, wanted some well-overdue revenge on the Vasquez's. So, he was also on board and setting up twenty-five large chemical explosives to take out each designated target.

After a long discussion over a feast of twelve-pound lobsters that Erica and Bianca brought on board from Nova Scotia. Everyone had an input on how these attacks were going to take place. Everyone had an intricate part to play as well. The ladies excused themselves, and we spoke as a family in more intimate detail about these attacks.

Jax: So, Dad, how do you feel about this situation?

Paul: Honestly, son, I don't know. I'm stuck on feeling hurt and thankful at the same time.

Jaylyn: Why hurt and thankful?

Carmelo: Yes, Unc. That sounds very confusing.

Paul: Hurt mainly because I thought running and playing it safe would make these issues go away. Hurt because I've been losing. Losing everyone I loved or cared for over street dreams as a kid.

Andrew: And thankful, why?

Paul: Thankful that one way or another, I'm going to give you guys the opportunity to live a full happy life.

Jax: Dad, you sound like you're not going to be here to see it for yourself.

Paul: I'm just ready for whatever. I'm ready to make that sacrifice to ensure each of your well being.

Andrew: Our lives are already fucked up, Uncle Paul. Look what we all had to endure as individuals and as a family. How I see it, we are all we have left. None of us want to see life without you.

Jax: Whatever sacrifices you have in your twisted mind, Dad…

Ana: Remember, we need you, and you need us.

Carmelo: That's as real as it comes.

Paul: Listen, I love each and every one of you to the moon. In my mind, my heart, and my gut, I'll do anything to protect your future. As a man, a father, a brother, an uncle, it hurts me to see what your fathers and I have done to you. What we caused to put your innocent lives at stake for our greed.

Jaylyn: You can't continue to blame yourself, Dad.

Jax: Dad, you're looking at the glass half full. Compare the life you gave us to your own. More better, yeah, millions of people who don't know wealth and riches.

Paul: We went from wealthy to straight greedy, and that was our problem.

Ana: Please let it go. None of us blame you. We love you, and if anything, we wish our families had just listened more. They would still be here.

Paul: You guys are making me super emotional right now. Let's just discuss these plans of attack.

The intel Erica gave us was that in two days, on Friday the 13th, the ships would be fully loaded and out to sea by 6 pm. The ship would use the cover of night to ease into their designated location's harbors by the following day. What we had in store by 1 am Saturday the 14th, all the Vasquez's businesses would be in flames. Erica had two of her people working on the docks. One of her men worked as a security on the ship dock. He was going to sneak Andrew and Alpha onto the docks as maintenance so they could get onto the ships. Once they were on the ships, they would plant the explosive devices through all the ships. Her other guy was the lead mechanical maintenance. He was responsible for getting the right documents and identification badges so that Andrew and Alpha could walk free onto each ship. He also supplied detailed maps of each ship, which Andrew and Alpha had 24 hours to study.

Andrew and Alpha had to report to the docks at 6 am sharp so that Erica's security guy could get them on the docks without raising any suspicion. Once they were on the docks, the security guy would drive them to the mega yacht first because it was the less guarded ship at that time. They would change clothes during the drive and hand over all the documents they would need for the job. They would also meet Erica's mechanic at the mega yacht, where he can assist them with the first two ships. Once they were on each ship, they had found their way to the engine room. Plant one explosive on the engine, another by the fuel and oil tanks, and the last, most importantly, in the bridge to ensure we take out the crew and captain of the vessel. Blowing the fuel tanks would ensure the entire ship would be blown into dust.

That very same day at noon, Bianca, Carmelo, and I would take a nice long drive south to San Pedro in a very nice Porsche Cayenne GTS. Once, we were five miles outside of the cocaine plant, we rendezvoused with Erica's inside man. Erica's inside man was a lady who ran her own irrigation company. She had us put on white tin cloth jumpsuits over our own clothing. This lady had a gasoline-sized water tank truck. A truck she used to water miles of plants, especially cocaine plants. The truck had six large, motorized metal pipes. Three on each side of the truck that extends sixteen feet long to water the plants. Andrew and I were going to hire new hires to help her irrigate roughly three miles worth of plants. Bianca had to sit tight for a few hours until we got back. This lady had her own personal vendetta against the Vasquez family. The Vasquez was responsible for her husband's death. He used to irrigate their cocaine plants for them for many years. One day, his truck malfunctioned, causing damage to a few yards of their plants. They didn't take into consideration his years of loyalty or work ethic. Instead, they made an example of him and killed him where he stood. Then the Vasquez's turned around and forced her to continue irrigation their cocaine plants.

Her name was Johanna Cruz, and we were going to help Ms. Cruz get her well-deserved revenge on the Vasquez family. Ms. Cruz was a much older lady who wanted to be free from this life. If I had to guess, I would say she was about fifty-five or closer to sixty. She was extremely strong and able for her age and drove this big water tanker truck like a twenty-year-old. From the moment we walked up to her, Bianca introduced her to us, and I could see the hurt and pain in her eyes. I could see the pleasure in her soul when we explained the detailed plan and the role she was about to play. She did not even seem phased about the amount of money we were about to pay her for her involvement. She just wanted to cause pain and destruction in Vasquez's world. We paid her a cool million dollars to empty her truck of water and replace it with very flammable plane fuel. We gave Ms. Cruz another three million to disappear and live a beautiful life for herself. She was grateful but also ready to die today if things went left as long as she was able to because of these roaches' pain. Her words, not mine!

Once we pulled up the plant, we were greeted by several guards who rushed out of the truck. They searched each of us and then the truck, in and out. Once they didn't find anything, they allowed us to proceed to the plant. Ms. Cruz knew of the guards very well. A young guy named Andres who she had a hand in raising. He quickly put a big, long AR-15 aside and greeted her with open arms. The two of them spoke briefly before we started to work. One of the guards made a great observation of the smell of the fuel. He asked Ms. Cruz in Spanish what that smell was. Ms. Cruz was quick and gave him an excellent answer without even thinking. She told him her truck had a bad gas leak earlier, and that was why she was late getting there. As we drove through the massive compound, Ms. Cruz discussed some concerns and her thoughts.

Carmelo: Damn, Ms. Cruz, that was a great answer.

Ms. Cruz: I already knew the smell would be an issue, so I knew I would have to explain why it smells bad.

Jax: Thank God you're quick on your feet, Ms. Cruz.

Ms. Cruz: The hard part of this is going to get these guards to give us some space when we start irrigating. The smell of the fuel is going to be intense.

Jax: That and the fact of planning these for explosive devices inside the plant itself.

Ms. Cruz: They don't let anyone inside at all.

Carmelo: We figured that as well. Our guy who designed these said two would do the job especially with this fuel.

Jax: We have a way of getting two of the explosives on the inside, so don't worry.

Carmelo: A little surprise in the bag right there.

Ms. Cruz: Andres can't get hurt is all I ask.

Carmelo: I'll handle Andres. I promise he'll suffer a bad headache.

Jax: Well, make sure they don't hold him responsible for any of this. They are about to lose, so much they won't want to lose anything else.

Ms. Cruz: OK, boys, let's cause these "bastards" hell.

We were followed by a black van, a pick truck, and a black Range Rover Sport for a mile into the compound. Ms. Cruz explained to Carmelo that they would be following us the whole time to irrigate the plants. Carmelo told Ms. Cruz to pull over for a second, and he jumped out of the truck. The two security in the black Range Rover jumped out, holding up their guns and screaming, "Que estas haciendo? Vuelve al campion agora. Vuelve al Camino agora. As they got closer to Carmelo, their tone got more aggressive. Carmelo held out a bottle of Aguardiente. Their whole demeanor instantly changed. Carmelo took a big gulp, and the guard's guns went from aiming at him to being strapped behind their backs. They were overly excited when they saw the bottle. Carmelo offered some to the guard who seemed to be in charge. He didn't hesitate to take the bottle after seeing Carmelo take a drink. He held the bottle up so the rest of his mates could see it. They also approached in a rather hostile manner for a drink as well. Before they could begin to argue over that single bottle. I handed Carmelo four more bottles of Aguardiente, and he handed them out to the men. The six men in the van took two bottles, and the three men in the pickup truck took two bottles. The guard in charge took a bottle for himself and the guy driving the Range Rover.

We waited ten minutes for them to enjoy a good, steady stream of drinking before we started spraying the plants. After twenty to thirty minutes of drinking, they slowly started drifting further and further behind us. With every thirty seconds, the distance would increase tremendously. Thirty-six minutes into drinking, we lost sight of the van. Three minutes after that, we lost sight of the pickup truck. Ms. Cruz asked, "Guys, what did you put in those bottles?" Carmelo smiled and answered, "Five bottles of two hundred chewable unflavored melatonin pills." Ms. Cruz replied, "That's a thousand pills in each bottle." Carmelo laughed and said, "It's enough to put a full-grown gorilla to sleep for a week," and we all laughed. A full minute later, the Range Rover came to a full stop, and all we heard was the horn
lowing loudly on the Range Rover. Carmelo screamed out, "oh Shit," and I told Ms. Cruz to "stop, stop, stop, and reverse quick." She didn't ask any questions. She knew we had to stop the horn from blowing before anyone on the compound would hear it. Once we were two car lengths from the Range Rover, Carmelo and I jumped out and raced to the Range Rover and pulled the driver's head off the horn. Carmelo and I laughed at the adrenaline rush we just had. We took the keys from the Range Rover, their machine guns, and all their extra clips. We ran back to the truck and reminded Ms. Cruz that we had just fifteen minutes to get this done before all hell broke loose. She just smiled and pressed a little button under the steering wheel, and the side

compartment next to the fuel tank opened. She said. "Grab those explosives, boys." Carmelo and I grabbed two explosives each. Ms. Cruz shouted out of the truck, "Good luck, boys," and smashed on the gas of the truck. The truck was spraying jet fuel everywhere.

Carmelo and I ran back to Range Rover. I pulled out the driver, and he pulled out the lead guard on the passenger side. I looked at Carmelo and told him, "You know what to do." Carmelo shook his head in disbelief and took off the guard's pants and shirt. He kicked the guard's dead, sleep-naked body off the dirt road and down a small hill into some cocaine plants. We jumped into the Range Rover drove towards the plant where the cocaine was processed while Carmelo changed into the guard's clothing. This was the moment of truth, so my heart was beating so heavily. To the point where I believed I could hear my heart beating in my chest. My hands got so sweaty fast, and Carmelo was breathing heavily like he had just finished running track. When we pulled up to the far side of the plant, where no one could see us. We encountered six more guards in the front of the facility. They were loud and had a good time among themselves. They didn't even notice that we had just driven up to the far side. Four of the men were sitting down cards, and the other two were standing over them and watching them play. I whispered to Carmelo that I would cover him from the other side of the building as he snuck in, hopefully unnoticed. Carmelo pulled out his iPhone and dialed my number. I answered, and we both put one earbud in our ears to hear each other. He said he was good, and I did the same. We gave each other a tight hug and wished each other good luck. Carmelo picked up the box carefully with his two explosives. I drove around the whole facility to the other end to cover him. I stopped at each corner of the facility to put an explosive on each end of the building. On one end was a huge industrial generator. On the other end, about fifty or so containers read (extremadamente inflammable), meaning extremely flammable. So, I squeezed my hand in the middle of a few of the drums and placed the last explosive I had. The facility was so big it took me four full minutes to make the drive. I got out of the SUV and walked to the last corner, where I could see Carmelo waiting in the distance. I got low and took aim from around the corner. I said into my earbud, "Melo, can you hear me?" and he replied, "Yeah, Jax." I told him he could go ahead but be extremely careful. I needed him to talk to me every chance he could so I knew what was going on inside. He replied, "Cool". Carmelo took a big deep breath, put on his big boy undies, and started to walk to the entrance with his head down. I was praying in my head that they wouldn't even see him as he walked right behind them. Carmelo told me, "Jax, I'm covering my face with the box." I told him to "keep your finger on the trigger of that gun just in case, cuz." Carmelo held the boxes up to cover his face and walked right by them. They were so caught up in the game that they paid him no attention whatsoever. Carmelo kept me in tune with every step he made. He described to me everything that was inside the facility.

Carmelo: Jax, this crazy. Bro, there are tons of people working in here, bro.

Jax: What do you mean tons?

Carmelo: Jax, there are women and children working in here. I don't know about this.

Jax: Are you shitting me?

Carmelo: Jax kids five, six or seven years old. We got to call this off I'm not killing no kids bro.

Jax: Melo, listen to me. Plan the explosives and I promise you I'll get them out before we blow the facility. But you have to be quick about it.

Carmelo: Cuz, please don't fuck me on this. We ain't no better than these people if we're going to kill women and children. Fuck that bullshit.

Jax: Melo, I just told you I won't be a part of that either.

Carmelo: OK cuz. I'm heading downstairs to the compressor.

Jax: There won't be enough time to plan the other explosive where they store the cocaine. Plan both explosives on each end of the compressor and get out.

Carmelo: OK, OK.

Jax: Imma start a diversion to not only get you out the front door but everyone else.

Carmelo: What? Diversion? What are you talking about?

I seriously started to panic. I did not know what to do. The situation went from easily planned to insanely overwhelming with doubts. Getting Carmelo out of that building was one thing. Now I have to get all of the people he described who were inside as well. What did we get ourselves into? He and I aren't ready to kill innocent women and children for our vengeful reasons. Carmelo was right about that, for sure. What would have made us any different from the Vasquez family if we were willing to do such madness like innocent murder? While I was caught up in my thoughts on trying to find a resolution to our problem, I heard gunfire very close by. I stood up and looked towards the main entrance. My heart literally skipped two beats when I saw three pickup trucks with loads of men with firepower heading toward this direction. I had seconds to come up with a plan to get my cousin and these people out. They were shooting their guns in the air and screaming out loud, "El completo esta bajo ataque." The compound is under attack. My Spanish isn't the best, but there was no way in hell I was going to wait around to find out what they were saying. The six guards jumped up from their card game and loaded up their guns as the trucks got closer. I had to think fast, and Carmelo started to panic as well when he heard the gunfire over the phone.

Carmelo: Jax, are you ok? What the fuck is going on out there?

Jax: For now, I am, but it looks like the cavalry is on its way.

Carmelo: I planted the explosive, but now get me out of here. I'm fucking scared as shit right now.

Jax: I'm working on it.

Carmelo: Working on it? Are you serious right now? We're so going die with these people.

Jax: Do you see any windows or a back exit in that place?

Carmelo: All the windows are welded shut with steel bars from the side.

Jax: I don't know what to do here, and in less than one minute, we're both dead.

Carmelo: Jax, find a fucking way, man.

My panic went to frantic. My stomach felt weird, like I wanted to hit on myself. I looked around, hoping for God to answer, and I saw the drums with the flammable signs. I looked up at the sky and blew a kiss to the heavens. I ran my ass over the drums and kicked over two of the drums over. I took the back of the AK, knocked off the seal, and put fuel out against the building. I lit a match and threw it against the building. The flames were high almost instantaneously to the point I felt my face burning. This was going to have to be the diversion we needed. The fires spread almost rapidly against the building. I told Carmelo to scream the (Fuego) out loud. Carmelo, of course, had to ask what does that mean. I told him, "Fire" and by that time, I said that the roof inside the building had started to fill with black smoke. Carmelo start screaming "fuego, fuego" over and over again. The people on the inside started to scream for their lives and run for their lives. I told Carmelo to run out with those people and keep his head down. He yelled, "Good plan" over all the screaming of women and children running for their lives. We had less than three minutes before we had to send a text, "Alpha," to blow the place.

As tons of innocent men, women, and children stormed toward the entrance of the burning building to escape. In fear, those people trampled over the six guards blocking the entrance. Carmelo was able to sneak by the guards with no problem. Of course, my petty cousin took the opportunity to kick one of the guards in the face as he ran by. He had a big smile on his face and I smiled back but from relief. I was able to get my cousin out. I grabbed Carmelo by the arm as if he needed extra help and we raced to the Range Rover. He was coughing a little from all the smoke. I checked on him and asked if he was ok. Then, I told him we weren't going to be able to make our escape through the front gate. He replied, "Well, find another damn way and quick before we all burn up." He was right; the flames had gotten the rest of the drums, and they started exploding one big bomb after another. It was only seconds before the flames would cause the explosive to detonate. I knew we needed some serious distance between us and that explosion. The flames got the jet fuel, and everything started to burn extremely fast. We never got the chance to text Alpha to blow the place up. In my mind, I was sure they could see these flames fifty miles away. We were racing in the opposite direction of the pickup trucks, and we heard a large, forceful explosion behind us. The force of the explosion lifted the rear of the Range Rover off its rear wheels and pushed the SUV a few feet. Women and children were running in every direction from the flames. Those flames were so high that they caused confusion for the guards. The smoke and flames made it impossible for them to see us or follow us. We heard one final explosion, and it was the entire facility. The explosion was so massive we stopped and got out of the SUV to look up in the sky at the flames. We jumped for joy cause the two of us were still alive, and we had just accomplished our mission. We just stood there for a good twenty seconds looking at the fantastic destruction we had caused.

I told Carmelo, "Let's go," and we got back in the SUV. At a short distance, we saw Ms. Cruz's truck heading toward the rear of the compound, so we decided to follow her. This entire facility was gated with a double fence to ensure no one could enter. Ms. Cruz's truck ripped through both fences like a hot knife to butter, and we just followed her. We headed north back to the mountains to rendezvous with Bianca. It was a quick fifteen-minute drive at eighty miles per hour up the mountainside. Carmelo and I were so amazed at how well Ms. Cruz handled that big ass truck. As we approached, we saw Bianca standing outside of her truck with a gun in hand. She ran over to us with sincere tears in her eyes. She was pleased we had made it out alive. She hugged both of us at the same time and cried. We didn't say a word. We just hugged her back for a few moments. Ms. Cruz parked her truck a few feet ahead on the dirt road and walked back toward us. She joined in on the hugs as well. Bianca thanked her over and over again. Ms. Cruz was crying as well. I can only guess she was relieved in her heart. She had a hand in striking a deadly blow in the Vasquez downfall. We all turned and looked down the mountainside and watched the flames burn miles of Vasquez's cocaine plants. Bianca walked away from us and toward her SUV. She opened the trunk and pulled out a large duffle bag. She handed it to Ms. Cruz and hugged her again. Thanked her so much for their help. She spoke to Ms. Cruz in Spanish (comenzar una nuevo vida de la que su esposo estaria orgulloso) "start a new life your husband would be proud of. Ms. Cruz just broke down crying. She hugged Bianca so tight Carmelo, and I could feel her pain. Ms. Cruz took her duffle bag of three million dollars in American cash, blew us all kisses, and got back into her truck.

We got back into Bianca's Porsche truck, and she drove off. Before I could say a word, she told us Erica and my father are extremely proud of us. She had already called them when she saw the flames from their compound. She had also sent a text letting them know we were safe when she saw Ms. Cruz coming up the mountainside. Bianca could not stop smiling at what we were able to achieve. Carmelo sat next to her in the passenger seat and asked what about the ships. She reached over with her left hand, held Carmelo's right hand, and said, "I thought you would never ask." She had her iPhone ready to show us a video of Vasquez's mega-yacht in flames, and we all laughed. The joy we felt was unreal that we were able to pull this off. Carmelo asked Bianca, "What about all the ships with the cocaine?" Bianca continued to smile even brighter. She told us from what she knew that all the ships went down at sea as we had planned. We had just put a serious financial dent in the Vasquez family's bank book. It was time to head back to the yacht to discuss the second phase of Erica and my father's plan. The plan would go from crippling Vasquez's empire to totally destroying each of them personally.

Chapter Eleven
The Game Is Chess, Not Checkers

I snuggled in the back seat of the SUV while Bianca drove. I kind of blacked out the chatter between her and Carmelo. I was physically and mentally exhausted. I kicked off both of my shoes and put my head back. I don't know how long I was asleep when I heard Carmelo's voice screaming, "Shit, shit, shit" and jumped out of my sleep. I sat up and asked, "What's going on?" Bianca pointed straight ahead, and Carmelo looked at me, and I said, "Oh shit." We were driving along Highway 25, which led us straight into Cartagena. It was a straight ten-hour drive. Without thinking about any blowback or repercussions, we drove straight into a roadblock. Bianca pulled off to the side of the road. There were about twenty cars ahead of us. From what we could see, there were five pickup trucks and four police cars. A bunch of men pulling people out of their cars, searching them and their vehicles. We watch them execute one man for resisting and asking questions. Hopefully, they hadn't seen us yet, so Bianca put the SUV in reverse to get us out of there. The only firepower we had was two handguns and a handful of bullets. The smartest thing for us to do is get off this road and hide till the morning.

Bianca and Carmelo were frantic and weren't thinking clearly. The two of them were talking about driving into a city and spending the night in a hotel. I had to be the mind of reason and remind them we are being hunted. If we saw police and henchmen stopping cars five hours up this highway. Think that they are pulling out all the stops. If I were looking for people who just took a billion dollars from me, I would be checking everywhere. I'm talking about hotels, bars, and restaurants all up these highways till someone can tell me something. We needed somewhere off the beaten path to hide and wait this out. Carmelo asked, "Where then?" I told Bianca to turn off the highways and take a path up into the mountains. I told them we'd be sleeping in the car tonight and to get comfortable. It was as if I was speaking Chinese. Bianca and Carmelo both looked at me, puzzled and lost.

Bianca: In the dark, black woods?

Jax: It's one night, and you live to see it tomorrow.

Carmelo: That's if we don't get eaten by a bear or mountain lion.

Bianca: I'm sure it will be fine, Carmelo.

Jax: Yes, Melo. And look at the bright side: You can snuggle up next to Bianca all night.

I just eased back in my seat and watched both of their reaction in the rear-view mirror. Bianca couldn't hide it; she blushed from ear to ear. Carmelo smiled to the point he had to look out the passenger window to camouflage his facial expressions and his body language. This confirmed my belief that they had real feelings for each other when neither one of them said a word.

We drove thirty minutes off a dirt trail into the mountains of nowhere before we parked under a huge tree. It felt safe up here, with crisp, clear air and a strong, smooth breeze. This was where we were going to spend the night. Camping out in the car. We were able to touch base with my father and Erica before heading into the mountains. I wanted to let them know we had Vasquez's people, as well as crooked police, after us. Erica had arranged to send some of her men to meet us in the city of Caucasia in the morning so they could escort us back to Cartagena safely.

We sat in the truck hungry but in great spirits, laughing and talking. After two hours of meaningless conversation, I found myself drifting away and into a deep sleep. I had the whole back seat to myself so I kicked off my shoes and snuggled up in the new leather seats. I was dreaming about simple things in life. Things I hope to experience soon without a care in the world. Eating at a hole-in-the-wall dinner with friends after enjoying a baseball game in the States. My life was strictly hundred-thousand-euro skyboxes with security. I was dreaming of experiencing as a regular everyday individual in the nosebleed section yet having the time of my life. They say that when you have been wealthy your whole life, you wish for simpler things in life. On the other hand, when you are poor, all you dream about is a wealthy lifestyle.

In my slumber, I could hear moaning. Moaning that kept getting louder and louder, forcing me out of sleep and to open my eyes. In the darkness of the SUV, I opened my eyes, which took a few seconds to focus. When I could see clearly, I saw Bianca half naked. She faced me, and I could only see one of her breasts. I closed my eyes again and reopened them for a clearer view. Bianca was straddling what looked to be Carmelo, who had his back towards me in the passenger seat. I didn't make any sudden movements to startle them to the fact I was awake. I stayed in the same position I was in to observe Bianca riding the shit out of my cousin. They were just a few inches from me, and these two were very sexual. I wasn't in the car with them. Carmelo had one hand over Bianca's mouth and his other supporting her back. Bianca had both legs bent and her hands around Carmelo's neck. Her eyes were closed, and Carmelo was having a hard time keeping his hand over her mouth. I just laid there playing dead as these two pounded each other out for the next twenty minutes.

Bianca couldn't keep it in when she orgasmed. Carmelo turned around to see if her loud moan had woken me. I quickly close my eyes, pretending to still be asleep. Bianca was mumbling quietly, "Oh my God, oh my God." I opened my eyes again very slowly to hear Carmelo saying, "Ah damn baby, ah damn." At that very moment, I couldn't help myself. I said, "Damn, that was good." Bianca screamed out her lungs and tried to cover herself in the dark. I couldn't help but laugh at the situation.

Carmelo: You son of a bitch. You were awake the whole time.

Bianca: You're sick, your fucking sick.

Jax: Wait a minute. Don't be mad at me. No one told you to risk getting caught fucking while my ass was in the car. Not too damn bright.

Bianca: You could have said something. Gross!

Jax: Nah, it was a great show. Your riding skills are perfect.

Bianca: You are so gross, Jax.

Carmelo: Not cool, not cool at all man.

Jax: I just hope you two used protection. I didn't see anyone pull out or unmount the pogo stick before you bust that nut, Melo.

They didn't utter a word. Instead, the two of them just looked at each other with a rather guilty look. Carmelo knew better, and in my mind, I was really hoping that they did use some form of protection. I can't see my cousin as a father any time soon. He isn't responsible at all. He was rather carefree, and he loved the party boy lifestyle. He was flashy and a playboy, and we all were. I couldn't see him giving that up anytime soon for wet, shitty diapers. Bianca asked me kindly to turn my face as she climbed back into the driver's seat and put her clothing back on. Like I wasn't watching them for the last fifteen minutes and saw all I needed to see already. In my gut, I did feel happy for the two of them. I wasn't sure if they had found love or just to fulfill their sexual desires. They were happy at that moment, and that was all they had right now regarding our current situation. Their smiles were big, warm, and real. It didn't take long for me to fall back to sleep with a smile on my face as well.

As the warm sun made its way through the thick tints of the SUV and warm face, I woke up before Carmelo and Bianca, who were snuggled in the front seat. Bianca had both knees to her chest, and Carmelo looked like his neck was broken. They were still holding hands. I opened the back door and quietly exited the SUV to relieve myself. I walked a few steps to the beautiful mountainside and looked down at how breathtaking Colombia was. I just stood there for a while, taking it all in. When I walked back to the SUV, Carmelo and Bianca hugged each other through the rear hatch of the SUV. Bianca sat with her back to Carmelo's chest, and he was holding her tight, kissing her neck. It was love; I knew that now. Before they knew I was in their presence, Bianca jumped and ran to the front driver's side of the SUV and grabbed her sat phone. As I walked up, they both saw me, and Bianca got off her call. She looked very serious and said her people were in place. We weren't going to be able to drive out of here. Carmelo asked, "Why"? And she answered, "The roads were all blocked, and the Vasquez's had hundreds of their own men, military soldiers, and police looking for us." I asked her, "How the hell were we getting out of here then"? She just smiled and said, "Trust me, now get in". I smiled and did just that. Bianca put that Porsche truck in an all-wheel drive and drove down that mountainside like the devil himself was chasing us. A few times, I thought we were going run into a tree and die, but her driving skills were impeccable. Someone had taught this woman how to handle a steering wheel well. We drove maybe ten or fifteen miles to the large open green field. As we were driving up, a black helicopter landed. Bianca hit the brakes hard, hit the park button, and said, "Run to the helicopter now." Carmelo asked, 'What are you doing"? She replied, "Baby, I'll be right behind you. I watched her hit the button for the gas compartment as we all got out of the SUV. My inquisitive mind wanted to see what she was about to do. So, I watched her closely. She ripped a large piece of her shirt, stuck it in the gas hole, and lit it. She then turned to us and yelled out, "Run," so I did just that. The minute we climbed into the helicopter, the SUV exploded. We all laughed as the helicopter took off.

Once we were in the air and we all had our headphones on, I felt safe. I asked her, "How the hell did this helicopter know where we were?" She didn't answer me; instead, she pulled out her sat phone, and Carmelo answered, "They could track us, cuz." Bianca added, "The pilot gave me coordinates nearby in that open field to rendezvous our pickup." I had to admit I was impressed with how she handled that. We all got quiet after that. I enjoyed the beautiful landscape of Colombia, and Bianca and Carmelo snuggled up and enjoyed each other. The flight was less than an hour, so I decided to close my eyes for a few.

Once we landed back on our yacht, which was now thirty miles from shore, my cousins and sister all came out to greet us. They all felt proud of us and what we accomplished. I asked Jaylyn where Dad was. She said, "He left this morning for Aruba." I was confused, and I couldn't quite grasp any understanding of why he would be heading to Aruba. That's when I heard Erica's soft voice. She said, "Jax, can I talk to you alone, please?" She looked overwhelmingly concerned. She reached out for my hand, so I gave her my right hand, and we walked away. We went back to her room, and for a quick second, I thought she was going to give me some congratulatory sex for a job well done. Instead, she picked up a well-folded paper and handed it to me. She said, "It's from your dad." She had tears in her eyes, so I knew it couldn't be good at all. With a deep breath, I opened the letter and began to read.

"Hi, Son: I couldn't leave today until I knew you were safe, and on your way back to your little sister to keep her safe. Jaxon that is exactly what I need you to do for me. Keep her and your cousins safe. I am depending on you, son, to do this and obey what I am asking you to do. This curse that I forced onto you kids is like a cancer in me. Slowly eating me from the inside, and now I need to deal with it alone. I can't ask anything more from you kids from this point on. You guys have done more than enough and more than any father should ever have to ask of his kids. I just pray as a father; I haven't failed you. I pray I haven't damaged your mental. I love you kids beyond words can express. Please forgive your old man for all the wrongs I have brought into your lives. Keep each other safe.

Your Loving Dad."

I was even more confused now. I didn't fully understand the reason for the letter or why he was going to Aruba. What I did know was that the letter sounded like he wasn't coming back. The only person who may have some understanding of what was going on was right here in front of me. So, I asked Erica what the deal was with the letter.

Erica: Jaxon, please have a seat.

Jax: Erica, please just tell me what the fuck is going on before I lose my mind.

Erica: Well, this isn't easy for me to relay to you. No matter how I try to tell you, it's going to hurt.

Jax: Erica, Erica, tell me, why is my father going to Aruba? What's in Aruba, Erica?

Erica: He is going to Aruba to fly to Spain.

Jax: And what the hell is in Spain?

Erica: Jaxon, please calm down. You're really scaring me.

Jax: I just need straightforward answers, Erica. So please don't beat around the bush. Tell me everything.

So, Erica held my hand and said calmly, "Jaxon, breath." The sincere, caring look in her eyes instantly calmed me down. She gently leaned over and kissed my hands, and my heart raced. She had my full attention when she said, "Jaxon, what I'm about to tell isn't easy." I asked her to lay out the entire situation for me. Erica said, unknowing to her, Yinnsely took a last-minute flight out of the country two days prior to us destroying her pipeline, ships, yacht, and cocaine plant. Yinnsely received the news while on retreat in Spain. Her son Andres broke the news to her that all of their fields, cocaine plants, and ships were simultaneously destroyed. Yinnsely knew someone was coming for her and her family. She knew this would cripple her. Erica had a guy planted inside Yinnsely's Colombian mansion. He had been feeding Erica information on Yinnsely for months. He said Yinnsely had ordered her kids Andres and Mila to fly to Spain out of fear to be by her side for safety. Before Erica's guy could relay this news information about the kids fleeing to Erica's people, the kids would be out of Colombia to be with their mother in Spain. They had a plane on standby and left in the middle of the night to meet her. I asked Erica, "Why Spain?" "Why would she feel safer in Spain as to Colombia, where she controls a whole army, the police, and her own men?" Erica smiled and said, "I'm about to get to that." Erica continued to explain that one of Erica's father's longtime friends had in-depth knowledge of Yinnsely's 9.9-million-dollar Pozuelo De Alarcon estate in Madrid, a home she purchased using a shell corporation she believed could never be traced back to her. A friend of Erica's father worked for Interpol. For years, he had been feeding Erica's family information and keeping close tabs on Vasquez's business and criminal activities in Europe. Her father's friend, Alvarado, even kept a detailed layout on her 19,000-square-feet mansion.

Since Yinnsely believed that her home in Madrid was purchased through a shell company that could never be traced back to her, she kept minimum security with her whenever she was in Spain. Alvarado informed Erica that whenever she checks in with customs using her Colombian or American passport, they immediately set up a surveillance team to track her every move while she is in Spain. Alvarado has been doing this for the past four years, and he told Erica she never has more than three to four men with her while traveling. Alvarado assured Erica her security details are structured as follows: A driver plus another security guard is in her car with her, and they are usually followed by a second car with two other guards. At her estate, there are another three security guards, not counting the other four in her convoy. The three other security guards worked at the home's front gate, and the last two handled patrols and camera surveillance.

With everything Erica was telling me, I was still confused as to why my father was in Aruba. Erica took a deep breath and said, "Jaxon, your father is heading to Spain. Before Erica could say

Another word, I cut her off and uttered, "He's going to kill her and the kids in Spain." Erica was speechless and just shook her head yes. I told her, "He can't do it alone," and Erica tried to reassure me he had help. Alpha was with him, and he was going to have help from Alvarado and Interpol. It was as if I completely blocked out anything Erica was saying. I immediately jumped up and walked out of her room. I heard her each time she said my name, "Jax, Jax, Jaxon." Each time she said it louder and louder. I didn't respond or acknowledge her calls to my name. I ran upstairs to the pool deck, where everyone was eating and having a relaxed, joyful time. I had one thought in mind, so I pretty much summoned Andrew and Carmelo to follow me. From the mannerisms and focused expression on my face, neither one of them questioned me. We walked off to the port side of the yacht, and with no hesitation, I discreetly told them about the situation with my dad. Andrew was the first to speak and asked. "So, when are we leaving for Spain?" I replied, "In the next twenty minutes," Carmelo asked, "are we going to assist him with whipping out the Vasquez family tree?" I said to them, "Your damn right, and to make sure he comes back to us alive." They both looked at each other and shook their head with full understanding. I told them to gear up the helicopter, which is taking us to Aruba, and we'll charter a jet from there to Spain.

Within twenty minutes or less, my cousins and I were ready to leave. We had our fake passports, clothes, and cash for four days. When I walked out of my room with my bags, Erica was waiting at the door. She had on a short silk black nightgown. She had no shoes or slippers. She looked worried and concerned. Before I could ask her if everything was ok, she lunged toward me. Grabbing hold of my shirt and locking her lips to mine. I was so caught off guard but pleased. I had wanted to kiss this woman since the first day she had her men aim pistols at our heads. We kissed for what felt like two minutes. Then she told me to please come back to her safely. I didn't want to promise her something I knew I couldn't control or had no say in. All I could do was shake my head yes with no words. She backed away from me, and I just watched her in silence. Once she left my view, I continued to the hangar deck where Andrew and Carmelo were already waiting. Jaylyn and Ana asked us to hold hands as we said a quick prayer for our safe return. The girls hugged us tight, and the tears rolled down each of our faces. They noticed Erica crying in the distance as well. The captain came down and hugged each of us as well and wished us the best of luck. I placed my bags on the helicopter next to Andrew and then ran to Erica to kiss her one last time before we took off. She laughed and cried at the same time. It was wonderful to have her arms around me and lips against mine. I told her I'd see her soon with certainty. This time, I walked away backward. I wanted to keep my eyes on her as I walked away. She was so elegant and perfect in my eyes. I wanted to remember this moment with her forever.

We waved continually as the helicopter took off. Trying to give off the possibility of hope and reassurance. The girls cried more hysterically the higher the helicopter got. The last thing we saw was the captain embracing Ana and Jaylyn to give them comfort. Erica just stayed to herself in the distance, crying as well. Within minutes, we were over the beautiful blue Caribbean Sea. Just focusing on the ocean was a sense of ease over my mind at that moment. There wasn't anything for any of us to say, so we all just kept quiet the whole time. Without thinking about it, we all pretty much did the same thing at the same exact time. Pulled out our air pods and popped them in our ears to listen to music to mellow ourselves out. The right list of music can do wonders for a person's soul. I looked out the window and just daydreamed of better moments in our lives. No matter what I did, and I'm sure I can speak for Andrew and Carmelo, that freight of what's to come was embedded in us. I'm sure we all did our best to relax our minds on this extremely short flight to Aruba.

Once we were over the Aruba airport, we all quickly got our stuff together to land for a quick exit. The helicopter landed only a few feet from the jet we chartered out of Aruba. The captain and co-captain, along with two flight attendants, were outside to greet us with champagne, caviar, and cheese bites. Usually, as men, we would all fight over the flight attendants to see who is going to score and take one or both down sexually during the flight. This, I can say, was the first time any of us was uninterested in those extracurricular activities. Andrew and I both grabbed a tall glass of champagne, and Carmelo grabbed the whole bottle as we boarded the plane. The helicopter pilot assisted us with our GoYard luggage and waved goodbye to us. I wondered if I would ever see him again. That when I realized how afraid I was. I didn't even know the pilot's name, so why I am wondering if I would ever see this man again. The pilot of our plane knew our delicate hurry, so no time was wasted on the takeoff. As the plane was ripping down the runway to take off, I received a text message from Erica. It was a 15-second video of her completely naked and playing in her sheets. My mouth completely dropped. My eyes have never been open so wide. Erica's body was absolutely amazing. Her small waistline and frame with perfectly thick curved hips. Hips that masked her huge Latin ass that looked like two watermelons. Most women are either blessed with ass or nice size breast. Erica was blessed with both. My mouth was watering. I wanted to turn this plane around immediately. In the video, Erica was telling me all of her and her body would be waiting for me to return back to her. If this wasn't all the motivation I needed, then nothing else is.

During this nine-hour flight, I must have watched this 15-second video over a hundred times. I thought to myself that I had never felt like this for any woman before. She had this Latin spark about her that drove me crazy. This was the first flight I had taken with my cousin where we weren't going to get charged an extra five or ten thousand dollars for destroying the plane. We were all mellowed out in our thoughts. Four hours into the flight, Andrew took off his headphones and asked, "How are you feeling?" I didn't really know how to answer him without feeling like a scared punk, so instead, I turned the question around on him. I asked him how he felt. He looked away at first and took a deep breath and said, "Scared as shit cuz." I replied, "We are in the same boat." I tried to reassure him we had help with Erica's people with Interpol. He even went as far as to tell him, "If it all works in our favor, we may reach my dad before he did. anything crazy." My father was the mastermind who did all our planning, so our trust was in him and him alone. I just knew in my guts we weren't going to be able to do anything without him. I told Andrew to do his best and get some sleep because we were all going to need it. He shook his head to agree with and gently placed his head back into his sleep and slept. I did the same thing.

Chapter Twelve
The Two-Headed Snake

I took two Tylenol-PM to help me sleep. I didn't open my eyes again until I felt that huge jerk from the plane's wheels hitting the runway. I kind of jumped up, a bit lost, and wondered where I was for a moment. Within that brief moment of wondering about my whereabouts, reality kicked right back in. We had just landed in the busy airport of Madrid, Spain. I felt a gentle hand on my shoulder, and I looked up to see one of the flight attendants smiling down at me. The other flight attendant was assisting with waking Carmelo and Andrew from their deep and well-overdue sleep. I smiled back at her to acknowledge I was awake. I looked out the window and past the airport to take in the landscape. I honestly loved this city deeply, I thought to myself as I looked out of the window. I have so many wonderful memories with and without my parents here, which made it extremely painful for me that my mother was gone. That pain turned into anger so fast that I didn't see the co-pilot standing right in front of me and telling us a customs agent would be boarding our plane shortly. That was kind of nerve-racking but not unusual at all. I wondered if our faces were on the news in Mexico, wanted for crimes that the Madrid authorities might not know about. My anxiety was high to the point the temperature in the aircraft got extremely hot.

For the next few moments while we waited, Carmelo, Andrew, and I did our best to relax. I was getting into my own head and putting thoughts that don't exist there. I'm pretty much psyching myself out. We were all facing each other from different angles on the plane. We didn't utter a word to each other. We just sat there in our own thoughts until I heard one of the flight attendants say, "Oh my God," as she looked through the window holding her chest. The shocking look on her face made us all nervous. The plane was just sitting on the runway. We lunged toward the windows to look outside. What I witnessed was four or five police cars coming toward our plane. The cars were coming from different directions. This was an unreal moment for us, especially because use I just jinxed myself with these exact thoughts. I wanted to tell the pilot to turn us around and take off. We were surrounded with nowhere to go, but in my mind, I felt we had a chance still to take off. I wanted to get us off here. So, I jumped out of my seat and ran to the cockpit to tell the pilot just that. I opened the door abruptly and caught both the pilot and co-pilot off guard. I immediately screamed at them to get us out of there. The plane was at full stop by this time. The pilots were taking off their headsets with disappointing looks on their faces. In a strong French accent, the pilot said, "My apologies, but we cannot." The police had the plane completely surrounded. The co-pilot explained they would also need EASA compliance to take off. Carmelo and Andrew were looking over my shoulder, shocked at the pilot's statement. They both were as confused as I was. We were all sharing the same two thoughts. Where the hell was all this heat coming from? Were we about to spend the rest of our lives in prison?

Carmelo: This has to be Yinnsely. It has to be!

Andrew: How the hell did she know we were coming?

Carmelo: It's like she has the Colombian police on her pay role. She has the Madrid police in her pocket as well. Come on now!

Andrew: What the fuck are we going to do? Jaxon, what are we going to do?

Jaxon: Nothing we can do but open the door and deal with whatever is about to happen like men.

Andrew: You think they are going to kill us or turn us over to Yinnsely?

Jaxon: No since wondering.

Carmelo: Or stressing ourselves out about nothing we can't control.

Jaxon: Time to man up if it's our time to go. We are going with our heads held high.

Andrew: Now you guys want to be gangsters. Ok Al Pacino and De Niro.

The three of us found our seats. I asked one of the flight attendants to bring me a strong drink. The co-pilot unlocked the door, and I could see the steps being latched onto the plane for debarking. It was a moment later when a man walked onto the plane. He was very tall with a long face. It was hard to guess his age, as if he was young and old, depending on how you looked at him. He took off his brown hat and grabbed my drink from the flight attendant that was meant for me. My mouth dropped, and I thought to myself this disrespectful bastard. I could just slap the shit out of him. He took one big gulp, held the empty glass to his chest, and tilted his head back like he just witnessed a slice of heaven. He then spoke sarcastically that he loved rich people while looking at the empty glass as he handed it to the flight attendant, indicating he wanted a refill. He then spoke again, called each of us by our full names, and handed each of us a very thick and heavy folder. He then took a seat and told us to open it. I was a bit scared and nervous about what I was about to find. It's a picture of Yinnsely and her kids. It was about a hundred and fifty pages of information on Yinnsely and her organization.

Andrew: Who the hell are you?

Alvarado: A friend of a friend, gentlemen.

Jaxon: How about a name, Sir?

Alvarado: My apologies, I'm senior inspector Alvarado.

Andrew: Erica's police friend!

Carmelo: We heard everything about you, but how did you know we were on this plane?

Jaxon: Erica told you!

Alvarado: Of course she did! Please don't be upset with her gentlemen. This was a smart move on her part to assist you with your task at hand.

Carmelo: Assist us, how so?

Alvarado: Well, I know your father is here in Madrid, Jaxon. I wish I knew where he was so I could assist him if I had known he was coming here.

Andrew: Senior inspector Alvarado, you still haven't told us how you plan to assist us.

Alvarado: Well, if you open the folder, I handed you, that would certainly be a start, gentleman. Inside those folders are detailed plans for Yinnsely's 12,000-square-foot mansion. All her recent modifications and reconstruction of her mansion. The folder also contains all the vehicles she currently owns and if there are any modifications or armored upgrades. Also, her right hand and best friend, Jazmine Lopez. Mrs. Lopez lives here in Madrid and handles 90 percent of Yinnsely affairs here.

Jaxon: Damn that's a lot of good intel?

Alvarado: Do let me finish! Don't be rude! You will also find Yinnsely's head of security and each of her security details, such as names, home addresses, soccer teams they play for, their kids' schools, his kids' names, wife or girls' names, occupations, etc.

Carmelo: WOW!

Alvarado: If you cannot find what you're looking for in there on the Vasquez's. Then it doesn't exist. Now, gentlemen, can you please grab your belongings? We must go!

Jaxon: Just where are we going?

Alvarado: I have arranged for you gentlemen to stay in the penthouse at the Four Seasons Hotel.

Andrew: I knew deep down I was going to like you. So, the Madrid police are paying for their stay.

Alvarado: Do not be absurd. My country will not fund your criminal activities.

Carmelo: Criminal! Activities! What the hell is this man talking about?

Alvarado: When you engage in actions such as blowing up ships, burning down fields, and carrying out hits, it constitutes criminal activity.

Jaxon: We are going to need three cars as well.

Andrew: Well, call it what you want. You push us; we push back harder.

Jaxon: Alvarado, we need really fast ones, two SUVs, and one four-door car that isn't too flashy.

Alvarado: I have a guy.

Andrew: A guy?

Alvarado: Yes, a Mr. Arturo Rodriguez. You can say he isn't doing 20 years because of me. He owns the largest BMW dealership in Spain. I will warn you. He only deals with the high-end BMW, and he won't be cheap.

Carmelo: I'm pretty sure we'll be able to afford it.

We got our belongs together and thanked the crew as we exited the plane. We found Alvarado had a large white sprinter parked right at the front steps of the plane. Alvarado opened the sliding door remotely with a key fob. Inside the sprinter were three of his agents working on a computer and surveillance equipment on board, some real double 007 stuff. Alvarado offered us to take a seat in the sprinter. I can't lie; I felt like a secret agent absorbing it all in. I wasn't the only one. Andrew and Carmelo felt that vibe as well. They were acting like schoolyard kids who just learned an exciting new game. Alvarado had our bags placed in two unmarked cars that accompanied us to the hotel. During the rider, we further discuss his role and what he brings to the table. I knew he was going to be a great assist. The man was the government. My cousins and I really didn't have any kind of plan per se. The information Alvarado presented us so far was a huge help. I told Alvarado we needed to find my father immediately. Alvarado informed us they had the most state-of-the-art facial recognition tracking system in the world. Alvarado and his team just needed two recent photos of my father and how the system worked. They promised their A.I. tracking system would get his location within three hours. Carmelo asked him how he was so sure they could find him so fast. Alvarado explained that their system is connected to every single digital video camera in South Europe using Wi-Fi. Andrew asked, "So all kinds of cameras then, like ATMs, traffic cameras, banks?" Alvarado replied, "Retail stores, taxis, train cameras, etc., etc., so yes. If it's digital and connected to a server, we can hack it and use that footage." Carmelo replied saying "Damn, being a career criminal is definitely not wise these days." Alvarado just smiled at him. One of Alvarado's team asked for my father's credit card information as well. I knew his American Express black card by heart, so I gave them that. I had no choice but to explain to Alvarado and his team that none of us were using bank cards or credit cards to stay off anyone's radar. So, the chances of my father using his American Express were unlikely. He knew using a credit card was a major red flag. Alvarado then assured me it was only a small piece to this puzzle of information they would use to find my father. A credit card wasn't really needed but would certainly help find him easier.

Within thirty minutes, we were pulling up to the Four Seasons Hotel. Two of Alvarado's counterparts exited the sprinter first. The drivers in the two cars grabbed our bags for us. We thank the
two, drivers Gaston, a tall spaghetti-frame young guy, and the lady, Gabriella, thick, curvy, and sexy in her two-piece agent suit. Carmelo and Andrew gave Ms. Gabriella a lot of attention, and she seemed to enjoy it fully. Alvarado interrupted their fun after three minutes of continued flirting and walked with us inside the hotel. He informed us he made a reservation four in the name of Michael Rosenberg. All three of us stopped in our tracks and just looked at him like he was crazy. I heard Andrew say, "Who the hell is a Rosenberg and do any of us look like a damn Rosenberg to you"?

Alvarado: We had to make reservations with this fake identification. We don't have hundreds of passports lying around to use. I have a pic of you, Jaxon, that Erica sent me of you. I used that picture to add this passport. You can use it to check into the hotel. They won't accept cash on check-in, so you will have to do a bank transfer to the hotel.

Jaxon: A bank transfer in the name of Rosenberg?

Alvarado: Your fathers have bankers all over the world. I'm sure you can work it out.

Carmelo: Can't you work that out, and we reimburse you?

Alvarado: Are you serious? This is an off-the-book job per se. You think Interpol is going to ok a whole hotel floor, including the penthouse, for thirty thousand euros a night.

Andrew: Wait, what?

Jaxon: Thirty thousand a night!

Alvarado: Yes, the whole floor is yours, and yes, thirty thousand a night. It's better that we have the floor to ourselves; no civilians will see anything we are doing or get in the way. I promise this will be under two hundred thousand Euros.

Carmelo: Oh, just under two hundred thousand. Sounds so easy when it's not your money.

Alvarado: Carmelo, seriously, you are wearing a two hundred thousand euro rose gold Patek Philippe Nautilus watch in solid rose gold. Oh wow, and Andrew and Jaxon. Seriously, serious!

Andrew: Seriously what?

Alvarado: A one-of-a-kind, twenty Richard Mille watch, that's what. Easily a million euros right there.

Carmelo: The man knows his watches.

Alvarado: Go and handle the check-in. My guys will head up with their equipment right after.

Andrew: Equipment?

Alvarado: You Americans really ask a lot of questions.

Jaxon: Our parents and family are American. We were all born in France guy.

After ten minutes of back and forth with Alvarado and stressing him out. We were able to check in using the fake passport Alvarado assisted us with. We needed to call Erica and Jaylyn to assist us with this wire transfer, something I nor Carmelo or Andrew had ever done before.

Jaylyn okayed three hundred euros for a one-week stay with a little extra to be safe. Once that was done and we could breathe a little easier, and we had a place to sleep at night. I didn't head upstairs right away with Carmelo and Andrew. I was a little hungry, so I decided to grab a bite at the hotel restaurant. I kept it simple and just ordered the hotel burger and sweet potato fries. I wanted to hear Erica's voice badly, so I called her while I ate. It was noon in Colombia and the girls were sailing back to Miami. When Erica heard my voice, she quickly jumped up and excused herself from everyone around her. I could tell she covered the phone but could still hear her telling them that she was heading to her room and be right back. I could hear Bianca's voice in the background saying, "Right, we all know that Jaxon is on the phone." Erica told her friend to be quiet as she hurried away from them so she could speak to me privately. I somehow could feel her smile through the phone. We never got the opportunity to be intimate. I seriously wonder if I ever will under these circumstances. Still, we brought each other joy and fulfillment. She must have told me she missed me twenty times or so in the first fifteen seconds of our conversation. I could barely get a word to ask her how her day was. It felt so good being on the phone with her. It was as if somehow, I was face-to-face in her presence. I kept telling her I missed her even more. The pressure of such a mental scare that I may not make it back to her was weighing heavy on me. It was a fear we both were sharing. I think at that point, I knew she was the one for me. I was beyond infatuated with her. Not a single second could go by without me thinking about her. She was everything I was built for but in the woman. A boss in every meaning of the word, beautiful, intelligent, and funny. In my eyes, she was the total package.

We spent four minutes on the phone after I ate. We just laughed at each other's little jokes. We weren't really talking about anything. It was as if we were living a normal life as boyfriend and girlfriend. I looked across the lobby and noticed Carmelo cuddled up on a sofa on the phone as well. I knew he was on the phone with Bianca. I told Erica that she and I weren't the only ones sharing a special moment on the phone right. She just laughed and said, "Let me guess, Bianca and Carmelo"? I replied, "Yes." I slowly made my way up to the suite where Alvarado and his coworker was setting up. Back to that James Bond feeling seeing all this state-of-the-art surveillance and computer systems. I just wanted to sleep till Alvarado spoke, "Jaxon, good news your father, we found him, and we think we know where he is staying. The facial recognition system has located him multiple times throughout the city. Our surveillance has shown him going in and out of the Mandarin Oriental Ritz hotel in the past day or so." Immediately after hearing that, I told Erica I would call her back soon. I turned around without saying a word and made my exit. Alvarado called out my name three or four times before the hotel room door closed behind me. I was on the elevator before he made it out the door to call me back.

Hit the lobby button, and a short ride down seemed to take forever, even though it was like thirty seconds or so. One of the doormen at the hotel spoke perfect English. I wasn't into any long speech or conversation. All I said to him was, "Cab to the Mandarin Oriental Ritz right now." He just shook his head, turned, and whistled. A cab pulled right away. He told the driver in Spanish where I was heading, and I was off. I rode to the hotel, playing so many different scenarios in my head about how I would greet my father when I saw him. I was praying he would be excited to see me and grateful I was here to stand by his side. But in my gut, I know he's going to be furious I am here with my cousins. I had to wrap my mind around the fact that my dad might kill me when he saw me. The wise thing for me to do was to be ready for the worst outcome as I exited the cab. I tipped the driver a hundred euros.

With my heart racing and the palm of my hand sweating. I walked into the hotel not knowing what to expect or the reaction I was about to undergo from my father. The Mandarin Hotel was a lot busier than the Four Seasons where I was staying. The line at the front desk was extremely long. So I walked to the concierges, in hope, I could just give them my father's name, and they would call his room for me. The first name I gave them they weren't able to locate him in their system. That was the same for the second and third names I gave them. I was a little embarrassed asking these people for different names and receiving an unwanted reaction of wasting their time. He was really annoyed, like I added the icing on his bad day for him. He replied to the gentlemen at the concierges desk, "Thank you a million." I felt bad, so I gave him a hundred euros and walked away. His whole demeanor quickly changed the minute the money hit his hand. As I walked away, he stated, "Sir, if there is anything else I can do to help you locate your friend, please don't hesitate to ask me, sir." I didn't look back or answer. I decided I was just going to sit by the entrance all night if I had to in case my father walked in or out of this hotel. The first two hours weren't bad. I ordered a large coffee pot, a fruit plate, and croissants. I wasn't even hungry. I just didn't want to be bothered while I sat there, so I tipped the waiter two hundred euros to be left alone as long as I wanted to sit there. The next thing I knew, my iPhone was ringing in my lap. I checked the time before I answered the phone. Three hours had gone by. The hotel Four Seasons was calling. It had to be Carmelo or Andrew calling me. So, I answered, and I heard Andrew's voice. He stated they had been trying to call me and text me for hours.

I told Andrew my phone service had been acting up since I landed. They were extremely worried and wanted to know where I was. Why was I gone so long? Why did I tell them? Why would I leave without them? Their questions just didn't stop. One question after the other before I could answer any of their concerns. I got overwhelmed instantly, and I just screamed into the phone I was fine, and I was handling something. Neither one of them said a word after that nor did. There was an awkward pause for 10 seconds before they both replied, "Who the fuck do you think you're talking to?" Carmelo screamed, "Jax I will whip your skinny little ass boy." I replied saying, "Carmelo, whatever man." Andrew said, "Seriously, cuz, where are you?" I broke down and told them I was at the Four-Season Hotel. They hit me with another question before I could tell them why I was there. Carmelo asked, "Oh ok cuz, you must have a nice piece of ass over there?" I replied, "No genius, I'm looking for my father," and immediately they hung up. I said hello three or four times before I heard the dial tone.
I wasn't in the mood for their bullshit at all. I turned my phone on its face and sat at the edge of my seat, waiting patiently. I was only focused on the elevator door, all three of the hallways, and the entrance.

A good thirty minutes had gone by, and no sign of my father. Through the front doors of the hotel came Carmelo and Andrew walking in, both wearing Louis Vuitton sweatsuits. Carmelo screamed out my name, "Jax," at the top of his lungs when he saw me.
I just dropped my head from the embarrassment. I wanted to run away from them like I didn't know them. Instead of running, I put my finger over my lips to shut their damn mouths from screaming across the lobby. They hustled over to where I was sitting. I pushed out two chairs so

they could sit down fast. Still trying to ensure they keep their voices down. Once they were seated, I asked them sternly, "What the hell were they doing here?"

Carmelo: Last time I checked, this was a team project.

Andrew: Yeah, this renegade bullshit you keep doing needs to stop.

Jaxon: Renegade! What the hell are you two talking about?

Andrew: Uncle Paul ran off to handle this alone and here you are doing the same damn thing.

Carmelo: This shit needs to stop. We came here with a plan that included all of us.

Jaxon: I hear, but this ain't about you guys right now.

Carmelo: You sound crazy, cuz.

Andrew: This is about all of us. We all lost family and friends through this situation. You can think for us or make decisions on Jaxon time. It's fucking us thing.

Carmelo: That's what it is, no exceptions.

Jaxon: OK, I can't agree with you. You're absolutely right. I was just trying to locate my old man.

Andrew: Well, cousin, there he goes.

I looked over my shoulder and saw my father exiting the elevator wearing all black and a hoody that he immediately pulled over his head. He knew there were cameras everywhere and didn't want to be seen or noticed. I quickly jumped and walked toward him, followed by Carmelo and Andrew. I didn't say a word once we were face to face. I had no words, but he was completely caught off guard. He froze in his step and looked around three or four times to see if anyone else was looking at or with us. His face immediately went from total surprise to instant upset. His first and only words to us were, "Follow me," so we did.

We walked back to the elevator and got on. My father didn't say a word, and neither did anyone else. We all just rode the elevator back upstairs to his floor. We walked behind him to his room quietly. My father placed his key card again on the security panel and gained access to his room. He walked in and held the door open for us. We all walked in one after the door. Carmelo was the last to enter the room, and my father slammed the door before Carmelo. Carmelo was the first to cop a plea.

Carmelo: Uncle Paul, before you get mad, this was Jaxon idea.

Jaxon: What?

Paul: Shut up, shut up. What the fuck are you all doing here? I gave instructions to stay put until I get back.

Carmelo: Again, Uncle Paul, I just want you to know this was Jaxon's idea.

Jaxon: Shut up.

Carmelo: Ain't going to be too much more of these shut up.

Paul: Why are you here?

Andrew: To make sure you come back to us.

Jaxon: You're all we have, Dad, and we can't lose you too.

Andrew: So be mad, be upset, but you're going to need Uncle Paul.

Jaxon: As a unit, we are stronger, smarter, and more equipped to handle almost any situation.

Andrew: Bianca has a whole Interpol unit in her pockets, and they are at our disposal.

Jaxon: Surveillance unit, tapping into any CC TV or cameras throughout the entire city. Things you can't do alone, Dad.

Carmelo: Listen to them, Uncle Paul. We know what we are talking about. That's why I told you we had to come.

Andrew: Shut up!

Carmelo: I'm shut up. I won't say a word after this. The disrespect is up here. Last thing, Uncle Paul, can I order room service?

Jaxon: Carmelo, you are special.

Andrew: Special Ed for sure.

Paul: Leave Carmelo alone. He just needs some puddling.

Carmelo: Wow, you too, uncle; the disrespect is real.

My father ordered up some food from room service for the three of us to eat. While we waited on our tomahawk steaks, we called our new friend from Interpol. The ever-helpful officer Alvarado will meet us at my father's hotel. Alvarado wasn't too far away, which was rather concerning to me, and I didn't share it with everyone else. I felt he was tracking us, but I also didn't want to sound too paranoid. Once she got to the hotel, we were pretty much finishing up our meals when he walked in. Alvarado really came off high and mighty based on his position

Interpol. Or maybe he just wanted us to respect him and what he represented. Alvarado introduced themselves to my father and told him it was an honor to meet him. Alvarado expressed his condolences for my mother and everyone we lost. With a very cocky tone he assured all of us that nothing like that would happen on his watch. My father shook his head and gave him a smirk. What was more disturbing was his knowledge of my mother and family's demise. I knew in my gut we needed him, but I didn't trust him at all. Before anyone could ask him where he got this information from. He was quick to let us know Bianca had let us know prior to our arrival. So, this mission was extremely personal to each of us.

Paul: So, Mr. Alvarado, my boys here tell me you're the inside man with all the answers and connection to help solve our issues.

Alvarado: Again, I understand this is personal to you on the highest level. So, this is for me. Erica's father is one of my dearest and closest friends. So, this is very personal for me as well.

Jax: I hear you, Alvarado.

Alvarado: Please, everyone, can call me Al.

Jax: Al, ok, Al, how do we know we can fully trust a man like you? We understand Erica's father was
friend, but how do we know you're not setting us up when this is all said and done?

A: Do you think for a moment I am not risking anything? I am risking my job as well as imprisonment if my superiors got wind of me using government funds and government employees to run an unauthorized operation.

Carmelo: Going to jail is a good point.

Al: 20 years!

Jax: It's a rather valid point. Still doesn't give us any assurance that we won't end up in jail as Well, to boost your agenda.

Paul: What my son is eloquently saying is what reassurance are you offering us?

Al: The only assurance I can offer is my word that once this is over you and your family can climb back on your beautiful private jet drinking champagne. I want the justification and full credit for capturing Yinnsely Vasquez.

Paul: There is one problem with that.

Al: And that is?

Paul: Yinnsely and her kids aren't going to jail. I'm putting her and her family in body bags.

Andrew: Toe tags!

Carmelo: Exactly!

Al: I am absolutely fine with that as well. We just have to go about it the right way so no unneeded questions or concerns about their deaths are asked. Again, gentlemen, I am not looking forward to any prison time.

Paul: Duly note Al.

A: So anyways, in the last three hours, we did some digging. Yinnsely's son Andres has been seeing this French model that lives here in Spain for some time now. Her name is Emma. Emma's brother Raphael relocated here as well in 2019 and opened a nightclub here in the city. It's an extremely popular nightclub, and Raphael does a lot of business with Andres.

Jax: Business? How exactly?

Carmelo: Drugs, I'm sure!

Al: Exactly!

Carmelo: They are drug dealers. What other business could they have been doing?

Jax: Shut up!

Paul: Boys, seriously!

Jax and Carmelo: Sorry!

Al: Yes, drugs. We've raided the club twice and came up with nothing really. I few patriots with the purest cocaine we have ever seen in Spain. Raphael just always seems to be one step ahead of us with the raids. About a month ago, we seized a truck from Lisbon to Madrid. The driver of the truck was transporting shrimp when a tire of the truck blew out. This caused the truck to crash and turn over. Three of the coolers carrying the shrimp exposed sixty vacuumed foiled bags hidden in the bottom of the coolers. The driver ran off of course and we found him and his family brutally murdered.

Andrew: How much exactly was seized?

Al: Over thirty million dollar's worth of pure Colombian cocaine.

Paul: Pennies! I'm sure that truck was a decoy truck. The Vasquez family doesn't leave witnesses or
coward alive.

Jax: They are that brutal, Dad.

Paul: Ernesto was loyal to the cartel for twenty years. They gave my friend his own distribution where he kept sixty percent of the gross profits he made. The Vasquez brother despised him for it. So, they came after him and us.

A: I know this is all very difficult for each of you. But if we plan this right, we can all go home and sleep at night without one eye open or seeing any prison time.

Paul: This is your city, and you're the man with valuable intel. So, tell me what you have in mind.

Al: Emma lives in a penthouse just a few feet away at the Hyatt residents. Raphael's nightclub is called Velvet Icon.

Andrew: Good intel so far.

Al: Whenever Andres is in town, he doesn't stay with his mother or at a hotel. The penthouse where his girlfriend lives belongs to Andres. They are inseparable and always be on each other's side. I have some people on my team tracking her and him as we speak. They are dining at Coque right now. As per Mila, she's a party animal and is at Velvet Icon every Saturday night and rents out the whole VIP section. On Friday night, she likes to party at Opium. On Sunday, she likes
to have fifty for her friends at her mother's pool.

Paul: God damn talking about 411

Al: What is this 411?

Carmelo: Old people's way of saying you got all the information.

Paul: Old? Really?

Andrew: It's kind of true.

Jax: Dad, your old man.

Paul: To hell with all of you. Continue Al.

Al: Yinnsely, On the other hand, has a different agenda than her kids. She loves the culture, the beautiful scenery, and the people. Yinnsely frequents designer boutiques, high-end art galleries, and concerts while she is here. Every other Sunday, she leaves the safety of her compound to eat brunch at El Club Allard, and every other Friday, she makes dinner at Ramon Freitas Madrid by herself.

Jax: So, we have a few good opportunities to bury Yinnsely and her offspring.

Paul: Very true, but I want her to lose both of her kids first to suffer. I am suffering. To be in agony like I'm in agony before I rip her black heart out.

Carmelo: Uncle Paul, you may want to sit on someone's sofa when this is all done.

Andrew: Yes, strengthen mentally.

Jax: Shut up.

Al: Are you people always like this? Sarcastic, pushing each other's buttons?

Andrew: Is it a problem for you?

Carmelo: Because we can act in a different kind of way that, trust me you won't like or appreciate.

Paul: Boys calm down. Mr. Alvarado, Al. My boys are young, and joking with each other is how they cope with their pain. They use humor.

Al: I see!

Jax: Back to the opportunities.

Al: Yes, so I was thinking it would be possible and relatively easy to catch Andres at the Hyatt

Andrew: We could easily catch him in the lobby.

Jax: The same way they did my mother and uncle Ernesto. Murdered on the front steps of a hotel and my mother in the lobby.

Carmelo: They are going to pay cousin, don't you worry.

As the night went on, the five of us spent hours drinking Dom Perignon and cooking an elaborate scheme to execute the Vasquez bloodline. After twelve hours of bouncing idea after idea off each other, we came up with a foolproof plan for seeing Yinnsely suffer like we have suffered. Alvarado also had information on four of Yinnsely's other relatives. Her aunt and older brother was in the great state of Houston, Texas. Her father was living a few miles out of Mexico City in Cielito Linda Assisted Living for senior citizens. Lastly, was her sister Adriana in Orlando, Florida, along with her family. Alvarado and his team had full details on everyone connected to Yinnsely. Her deceased husband and his brother's families were wiped out in the late 80's and early 90's by the hand of Yinnsely. She wanted full control of the production and distribution of cocaine out of her region of Colombia. So, with one order, she murdered everyone she believed would undermine her authority.

I taped out around 4 am and called it a night. I wanted to hear Erica's voice before I closed my eyes and dreamed about her. We had a quick fifteen-minute conversation of laughter and smiles.

Before I knew it, it was noon, and Andrew was shaking me and shouting my name, "Jax, Jax, wake up." I jumped out of my sleep and to my feet, thinking something was wrong or that we were in immediate danger. Only to find Andrew looking at me as if I was crazy. Once I was able to relieve myself, wash my face, and brush my teeth. I made my way into the living room, where my father was sitting with Alvarado and two of his associates. They had great news to share with us. A Mr. Nicolas Gonzalez was apprehended at 6:05 am that very morning. We were all puzzled and confused by this news because we had no clue who this person was. Alvarado explained that Nicolas was Yinnsely's financial adviser and lawyer. He was also head of one of the biggest banks in Singapore. Alvarado believed he had full control of Yinnsely's money all over Asia and Europe. I won't lie. This was like heaven music to our ears. Alvarado wanted my father and myself to firmly talk to Mr. Nicolas in our own way if we were somehow placed in a room with him. I couldn't wait. Andrew and Carmelo weren't too pleased with not having a hand in interrogating Mr. Nicolas. Instead, my father gave them both an assignment to handle before the day was over. I rushed into the shower with enthusiasm, so I didn't hear what the assignment was. I got dressed quickly in the same clothes I had on the night before since we stayed at my father's hotel. My father was two minutes behind me, so we could head out with Alvarado or Mr. Al. We climbed into his Sprinter truck, and we were off. We drove maybe ten to fifteen minutes to a local police station where their chief officer was a personal friend of Alvarado's. Al greeted the chief, and a few words were exchanged. Then, he signaled that my father and I should follow them. We met up at a group of big red steel doors, and some more words in Spanish were exchanged between the two men. Al placed his right hand over his heart before the chief handed him a set of keys and told his two other officers to walk away. The moment they were out of site. Al told us we had ten minutes to extract any information we could from him. He told us Nicolas spoke perfect English and French, so we wouldn't have any issues understanding him. My father asked, "Why only ten minutes?" Al explained the chief was going to conduct a video surveillance test of their systems, which took ten minutes. Once the system comes back up, we can't be seen in that room with him. His face can't be damaged either for the cameras. He went even further to explain that all police surveillance systems feed straight into a hub along with twenty or so police stations throughout Spain. Their only job is to watch these cameras 24/7. I was a bit worried, but with total confidence, my father told Al we would only need five minutes.

Personally, I wasn't sure how my father was going to go about getting the information we needed from this man without showing any physical scars or damage to his body. At that moment, Al's phone rang, and he answered it with a concerned look on his face, and he then said ok. He looked at us with a now anxious look on his face and said, "Go, go," and quickly opened the steal red door. My father had a small backpack with him, and no one knew what was in it, and no one cared to ask either. I was beyond nervous now. Knowing we only had ten minutes and we couldn't get caught on camera was extreme pressure on me. My father said very calmly, "Jax, help tilt his chair over so his feet are in the air and take his shoes and socks off." So, I did just that. Nicolas was handcuffed to the chair and blindfolded. He started struggling and fighting. My father pulled off his blindfold and immediately started threatening me. He wanted us to know who and how important he was. What could he do to us for treating him like this? My father placed his hands over his mouth to shut him up. He looked Nicolas in the eyes and told him very nicely that he wanted full access to all Yinnsely Vasquez's accounts. The eye on Nicolas grew extremely large and wide. My father removed his hand from his mouth, and Nicolas laughed and threatened us again. Saying Yinnsely Vasquez would bury us and our entire family, even the family dog would die. My father then reached for the backpack and pulled out a drill and then an extremely long gold color drill bit. My father told me to hold down his left leg firmly. Paul told Nicolas I'm going drill a hole into the bottom of your feet and straight up into your leg. He explained to him that he would easily bleed to death in seven minutes. Nicolas replied, "You don't fucking scare me. I know you're bluffing." So, Paul started to drill. He drilled about an inch into Nicolas's feet before he complied to do whatever we needed him to do.

My father banged on the red door so Alvarado could open it. Alvarado opened the door with a puzzled look of disbelief that there was no way we got this man to talk so fast. Paul asked Alvarado to retrieve Nicolas's laptop from his personal belongings. But Alvarado was only focused on the fact that Nicolas was crying his eyes out and begging for help. My father asked Al to snap out of it, and he did. Al told one of the officers to hurry back with the laptop. I looked at the time on my watch, and we had seven and a half minutes before those cameras would be turned back on. Al was at a loss for words, looking down at Nicolas with blood running down his feet. Then Al asked, "Is that feces I smell?" I replied, "Yes, I think Mr. Nicolas shitted on himself." My father asked one of the officers to get him some bandages to wrap his feet. The officer complied and took off running. It was only moments later when another officer came running with the laptop. I looked down at my watch, and we had five minutes and fifty seconds left.

We gently sat Nicolas back in his chair as an officer dressed his foot and placed his soaks and shoes back on. Nicolas opened his laptop, and his fingers went to work. Yinnsely had four accounts with his list of financial institutes. Yinnsely thought she had crossed her T's and dotted all i's and lower-case j's when it came to protecting her money. She had over eight hundred million
in Coast Rican account. There was another one-point-one billion in the Bank of Spain and nine hundred million in a bank in Zurich. The largest majority of her finances was in Singapore. She had just over three and a half billion dollars and a half billion in gold investment.

Nicolas was begging us not to kill him the whole time, and my father, Paul, just kept telling him to focus with a firm grip on the back of his neck. The smell coming from Nicolas was really bad. I wanted to vomit so bad. With his eyes full of tears, Nicolas asked for my father's cell phone. He explained that he was encrypting his cell phone with all of Yinnsely's accounts. He opened a back door into each of her accounts and linked everything to his phone without anything coming back to him. Nicolas explained that the moment Yinnsely logged into any of her accounts, we would receive an alert with her twelve-to-nineteen-digit passwords. Once we logged into her individual accounts, we would have full access to her funds, and she would be permanently locked out of her account. She could only get back access by getting on a plane and visiting each bank or with Nicolas's help to get back into her accounts. We didn't trust Nicolas, and we needed him to spend a few more nights in these walls. The police chief assured us he could hold Mr. Nicolas for a few days longer. Seeing that he had no identification on him when he landed privately in Spain with questionable substance. Substances that needed to go to the label for testing.
We all smiled at each other, and my father gave the chief a very fat envelope for him and his officers who assisted with this situation. We expressed our utmost gratitude to Al and Chief for

this small win. When I asked Al on the way what that substance was, he smiled and answered Tylenol. These cops were so dirty, but I loved it.

Within a few hours after leaving the police station, we received our first alert. Yinnsely accessed her Singapore account, and my father smiled from ear to ear. We were back at our hotel, updating Andrew and Carmelo, how much progress have we made? We watched my father transfer one billion of Yinnsely money to a cancer association, an abandoned kids association, a heart association, and ten European universities. The rest was transferred into our Cayman Islands accounts. My father loved this. The following day, Yinnsely's Zurich and Coast Rican accounts were completely emptied right afterward. Her account in Spain wasn't accessed online at all. Four days had gone by, and we were just waiting for her to access it so we would get that alert, but it never happened. We had Al call the police chief to question Nicolas on what was going on with her account here in Spain. In less than twenty minutes, the chief called Al back to inform her that she was on to us. She transferred all of the funds into a cryptocurrency, which was going to be impossible for us to access. We were fine with that. We had just taken billions from her and knew it was a huge stable for her.

Chapter Thirteen
Caught in a Deadly Web

Now, it was time to move forward with part two of our elaborate plan. With careful planning and detail, we knew where Mila and Andres were going to be and what they would be doing over the next few days. So, we made proper preparations to pay them a visit. We all had a part in this task, and by noon, I was parked outside the Hyatt with Carmelo behind the wheel of a limousine-tinted black BMW M5. We needed something super-fast and agile but didn't stand out too much. The M5 was the perfect car for what we needed to do. Across town, my father and Andrew were tracking Mila and a group of her friends. They were hoping from designer stores to little high-end eatery spots. Timing was everything we had planned for them. Andres and his girl didn't leave the Hyatt till 6 pm, and honestly, we were getting tired of waiting on them. Andres came out not only with his girlfriend but two bodyguards. This was unexpected, for sure. I called my father right away to tell him we may need to rethink this situation. In turn, he told me they had the same issue. Mila was with five of her friends, but there was a black Range Rover Sport following her every move as well. They had to pull back and keep their distance so as not to be noticed.

My father then told me he'd call me right back. While I followed Andres and his girl Emma on Foot, they held hands and walked down Calle De Breton De Loss with security close behind. It was a short walk to a pub called Bodeguita De Enmedio. Carmelo waited for me to call him and tell him where I was. As they were walking inside, my father called me back. He informed me that he gave Al the license plate of the Range Rover and its current location. Al and his team were now tracking the Range Rover using traffic cameras, nearby ATMs, and city CCTV cameras. My father wanted to keep his distance until he was ready to act. He wanted me to be extra careful. I walked inside, not too far behind Andres and his girl. The manager was overly excited to see Andres, and the two exchanged hugs and cheek kisses. I walked over to the bar and ordered a drink while keeping a really close eye on the situation. The manager brought Andres to a VIP section that was roped off for all to see. Andres thanked the manager and gave him a tip before they parted ways. Andres did not sit down with his girl; instead, he made his way to the restroom and followed. I thought this could be the opportunity to grab him.

My father ended up only a few blocks away at the Louis Vuitton store, following Mila. To his surprise, Mila's security got really tired of following him from store to store for hours. Instead, they decided to park right outside and keep a close watch. My father and Andrew decided this was their opportunity. My father reached into his glove compartment and pulled out a 357-snub nose and placed a silencer on it. The street was a very busy street with lots of people walking around, but my father took this as an advantage. He had Andrew rear-end the Range Rover just enough to leave a small dent. Nothing loud to draw the crowd or anyone's attention. My father exited the van and walked past the Range Rover. Andrew placed his silencer on his Glock 17 and proceeded to drive slowly toward the Range Rover.

I followed Andres into the restroom, hoping his security would give him his space. But of course, one guard stayed with Emma, and the other followed Andres. I walked in, and his guard was standing to the left of me as I entered the restroom. Andres was in a stall handling his business. I

was so grateful for the music being extremely loud. The walls of the bathroom were shaking. I prayed
no one else walked in until I was done with this situation. I walked over to the sink and washed my hands. Looking in the mirror, I was sizing up the guard. He was 6 foot 4 and 240 pounds easy. This guy was all muscle from steroids. I had to be smart, quick, and heartless if I wanted to survive this freak of nature. I reach for the 6-inch razor edge knife I had in my back pocket. Then I dropped a stack of cash on the floor right in front of the guard to distract him.

My father gave Andrew the ok to rear-end them once he was ready and no real witness to see what was about it take place. My father stood in the doorway where he could see the passenger of the Range Rover right across the street from them when boom. The van hit the bumper. The driver and passenger both jumped out, shouting in Spanish, "You fucking asshole, you dumb fuck." The driver of the Range Rover walked up to Andrews demanding that he lower his window.
The passenger walked up to the passenger side of the van banging on the window. Clearly, he didn't see my father walking up behind him with a hood over his head. Andrew lowered his window slowly and with a smile on his face, which infuriated both men.

While I had this rather huge man distracted, I seized my opportunity. He quickly reached down for my money as if it were his. So, I decided to strike at that moment. I had to be lightning-fast with this knife. His head was down, so I stabbed him in the neck twice. The blood just exploded from his neck. He quickly grabbed for his neck. He tried his best to look up at me. Instead, I grabbed his head, and with all my force, I kneed him right in the neck I had just stabbed. The force I hit him with completely knocked him to the floor. The moment his body hit the floor face down, I reacted. I rushed to his left leg before he could quickly recover. This was a big dude, and, in my gut, I felt the stabs in his neck weren't going to be enough to keep him down. With the knife in hand, I stabbed and sliced his inner thigh, destroying his artery. It didn't matter how big or how strong he was. He would bleed out in ten seconds to his death.

As the two men began to get really pissed off, the guy on the passenger side of Andrews van raised his hands in anger and he froze. His eyes rolled to the back of his head, and he dropped to his knees with his hands still in the air. The driver of the Range Rover was puzzled on why his passenger had just dropped to his knees. It took the driver five or six seconds to realize Paul had just shot his passenger in the back. The driver tried to reach for his gun before his passenger's body hit the floor, forgetting about Andrew in the van with his window fully down. Before the driver could get his feet in a proper stand and take aim at Paul, Andrew had released two shots at the driver, hitting him once between the eye and the other in his chest. Andrew jumped out of the van and looked around for witnesses. People on the street were too caught up in their own world to notice anything at all. Paul grabbed the passenger's body and dragged the body to the back door of the van. Andrew opened the side door of his van and hurried the driver of the Range Rovers body and dragged the body to the van. They both shoved the bodies into the van and took another looks around for witnesses, but to their blessings no one noticed.

Just looking down at the body of this 240-pound bodyguard lying on the restroom floor shaking in front of me. The blood just poured from both his neck and leg. I watch his eyes slowly come to a close. I gathered myself together and walked over to the stall Andres was in and waited. When Andres exited the stall, he saw his bodyguard's body dead on the floor. He instantly began to panic and saw me standing in the mirror behind him, dripping with blood on my hands. He tried to scream so punched, and he flew to the floor. Knocking him out completely. I called Carmelo, panicking to let him know I had Andres. That I had knocked him out cold on the restroom floor. He told me, "Cuz look if there are any windows in there and there were. He told me there wasn't anywhere to pull the car up closer, but he would walk over to the window quickly. I opened the window and looked outside to make sure the coast was clear. It had begun to pour down rain. I could see Carmelo running toward me, drenched from the rain. Carmelo reached into the window to assist me with Andres as I lifted his body out the window.

Paul walked casually into the Louis Vuitton store and asked for the VIP, personal shopper assistant. The store representative asked my father if he had reservations set up for a personal shopping experience for today. My father didn't say a word in response. Instead, he just pulled out his American Express black card and gave the representative his back, like how dear you ask me if I had an appointment. That black card meant unlimited spending, so the store was his, and they couldn't afford not to assist him. All he heard from the representative was, "I'll have someone assists you right away, sir." As the personal shopper walked my father to his VIP room to shop in peace, Paul walked right by Mila's VIP room. Mila and her friends were drinking champagne, laughing, and having a great time. My father didn't want to spend a lot of time in the store, especially with all these video cameras and security. My father told his personal shopper he wanted a full quick order on a six-piece men's travel set and just handed her his card. In exchange, she handed him a glass of champagne. He told her to make it quick and have it delivered to his hotel under the alias he was also registered with at the hotel. It took her five minutes, and she brought him a very detailed receipt. He placed his glass down, pulled his hat lower to cover his face, and made his exit. The moment he walked out of the store, he looked at Andrew and nodded his head. Andrew then dialed a number and heard a small explosion inside the Louis Vuitton store. There was so much smoke, and everyone inside the store came running out coughing and covering their eyes from the burning smoke. My father stood to the side of the main doors and waited. It wasn't long before Mila and her friends came running out as well with their heads down and coughing. Without anyone noticing, my father grabbed Mila and injected her with Midazolam in her neck. Her body instantly became almost lifeless. Her eyes were half open but totally helpless, and he easily picked her up and carried her to the van. The smoke was strong and thick. People could hardly see or breathe, so no one noticed my father carrying Mila to the van. My father closed the rear door to the van with him and Mila inside, and Andrew drove away.

Carmelo and I had a little bit of trouble carrying Andres to the car before we could drive away. We couldn't stop high fiving each other out of straight excitement. The adrenaline that was running through our veins was intoxicating. The high of what we had just accomplished was amazing. I called my father immediately to let him know we had Andres knocked out and tied up in the back seat. Paul was calm but proud over the phone. I could sense the mixed emotions through the phone. Dad hated the fact he had us in this situation but was proud of how we were handling it. He told us to be safe and to hurry to the abandoned auto shop where we planned on stashing both Andres and Mila.

At our little hideaway, the auto shop. We had Andres and Mila on separate sides of the shop.

Both of them gagged and blindfolded. They both were tied to a chair on just two legs, dangling.

We had a massive size chain around their bodies that was connected to the ceiling foundation. Just one wrong move, and they would be hanging six inches from the ground with the chain crushing their arms and eventually their lungs. We took two 30-second videos of the two of them in case we needed to send a frightening shock down Yinnsely's heartless back. Her kids were her world, and my father certainly wouldn't think twice about taking their lives to crush Yinnsely. Now, it was the second part of my father's plan, and it was simple. He was going to turn the tables on a cartel boss's wife. Show her for once how it feels to receive a finger or lips of one of her children in the mail. Something these cartel devils find pleasure in torturing their rivals.

He told Andrew he wanted the video of Yinnsely kids on a Zip driver and to find someone to deliver to her favorite restaurant where we knew she would be dining in the next hour. My father was hoping Yinnsely would call his bluff. Andres had a tattoo on his left shoulder of a dragon wrapped around a human skull. My father had the largest potato peeler I had ever seen in my life. That potato peeler was going to be used to peel off the tattoo on Andres' shoulder and send that to Yinnsely to show her we weren't playing with her. My father wanted to cripple her, take everything away from her before she even knew what was taking place.

We hired a carrier service to deliver the Zip drive and a note with a number at which Yinnsely could reach us. After two hours had gone by, we got no call, and since the carrier service couldn't be linked back to us, they couldn't call us to confirm delivery either. This started to stress my father out intensely. I decide to call the carrier service for an untraceable number. The gentlemen on the phone didn't speak the best English, but we got by. He made it clear that the carrier had returned with the package. Stating the receiver wasn't at the location today. The only explanation we could come up with was that Yinnsely was now paranoid. One of her major accounts were seized, and her money was gone. My father, in a rage, kicked over a table and destroyed two chairs. We didn't say a word or try to stop him. We fully understood his pain and anger. But then he smiled. Yinnsely accessed another one of her accounts in Spain and Zurich to ensure she still had those funds available. My father looked up at us and said. "We got that bitch now."

Carmelo: Uncle, which account did she access?

Paul: Her dumb ass gave us access to both of her accounts.

Andrew: So, let's empty them out right now.

Paul: No, let's wait till tomorrow. I want her to wake up fucking broke and lost in this world.

Jax: Her money is her lifeline. Without it, she was hopeless and helpless.

Paul: She has no friends; her kids are her only family.

Andrew: Uncle Paul, I must admit I'm still really nervous about what we are doing. I just don't want this blowing up in our faces.

Paul: I never asked anyone of you to follow me on this journey. I wanted to do this alone. This is all my doing. Now you're all here so you're either going to man up or bring your asses back home.

Jax: Dad, Andrew isn't saying he's not going to follow through.

Paul: Andrew can speak for him damn self-boy.

Paul was beyond serious about everything that we were putting into play. He wanted Yinnsely face down in a pool of her own blood. Buried in the ground with her husband and his brothers. He made statements like I want to bury her with her head up her own ass. I'm going to burn that bitch alive on a steak. My favorite was tying a rope around her neck and having a donkey drag her through her own village. Some real off-the-wall statements had us puzzled half the time. I knew he was hurting tremendously. He loved my mother deeply to his core. He wasn't ready to lose her, and not the way he did. He lost his closest friends, his brother, cousins, and kids he considered his nieces and nephews. He wanted anyone who had a hand in their demise dead. My mother was everything to him, and no one couldn't tell him it was not his fault she was gone right now.

Paul: With Yinnsely money in our position, I'm sure she is beyond desperate at this point. Confused, worried, and beyond desperate.

Jax: Dad, I wouldn't understate Yinnsely.

Andrew: Cuz, we have everything she loves, her kids and her money. She's clueless right now.

Carmelo: Uncle Paul, with all due respect, I am in no way underestimating you right now. Do you
really think that's enough.

Paul: Yinnsely is that one percent.

Andrew: One percent of what?

Paul: She is a woman who only knows luxury, status, and the finer things in life. She has been rich for so long that she is no survivalist. Trust me, kids, I have done my due diligence. She cares for her kids, but she loves her money.

Jax: Without her billions, she won't have any support from anyone. She's helped put countless families in the ground. A lot of people want her dead.

Paul: Tomorrow is the day kids, tomorrow we get this done.

The following morning, everyone was up extra early. I don't believe anyone got any sleep for sure. Andrew was on his third cup of coffee. Everyone gathered in the small hotel kitchen in my father's suit. Everyone was just sitting there quietly in their own thoughts. I asked my father to pour me a coffee, and he just looked at me with a very humble smile. He placed a hand on my shoulder and whispered, "It's going to be ok, Jax." I just smiled back at him and shook my head. But deep down, nothing felt right. This wasn't going to be ok at all.

At roughly 6 am, some of us had on tactical gear. Carmelo and I dressed in Movistar cable uniforms. By 7 am, Paul, Andrew, and I loaded up our equipment in the cable van.
We had a short drive to rendezvous with Al and his people. They couldn't physically assist us besides using their surveillance equipment, which would help keep us two steps ahead of the opposition. After a brief meet and greet, we will discuss the details. We were off to our destination. The plan was to get onto Yinnsely's property as her cable company. We knocked out her internet and cable the day before. Al and his people intercepted the call from the cable company. It was just our luck that our hotel was redoing its entire security, internet, and cable through the building. So, no one was going to miss one of their fifteen vans for a few hours.

Yinnsely had a lot of security and guards overlooking her compound. But with the internet out they had no cameras working, so this made her extremely nervous. What we didn't know was she was packing to flee the country. The guard at the gate was happy to see us when we pulled up. He thanked us five times for coming so early. He expressed that the owner was starting to stress everyone out because the cable was off. I'm just glad Carmelo was fluent in Spanish. One of those things he did was take the opportunity to learn while growing up with Uncle Ernesto and his family. The security guard quickly opened the gates and gave us access. We drove up to the compound, and there was a guard standing by the front doors. He waved us over to pull up right in front. In Spanish, he told us the internet is out, and they have two separate boxes. One was located inside the house, and the other in the garage. We told the guard we needed to see the box inside the house first. He acknowledged our request but asked us to open our toolboxes to view the contents inside. He took a quick view of the tools on top. As he attempted to reach into one of the toolboxes, Carmelo interrupted him by stating in Spanish that this was time-sensitive and that his boss wanted this done in a rush. He took a good, long look at us both. Carmelo was chewing gum and blowing bubbles. I, myself, am wearing these big nerdy glasses. We looked like pencil-pushing internet-surfing geeks. He told us to close the boxes and to follow him. But first, he asked us to turn around and face the trees with his hands up. He did a quick pat down to make sure we were armed or carrying anything. He then led the way into the house. Telling us in Spanish not to touch anything.

Once we were inside the house, Andrew and my father sneaked out of the cable van, both heavily armed and processed to cover the premises. My father found a tall tree to climb with a good line of sight, covering the whole property. With a sniper rifle and full camouflage attire, he took aim to cover us. Andrew sneaked past Yinnsely, and other guards covered the grounds of the house. Some were just too busy on their phones to even notice him. He made his way to the rear of the house and hid. He patiently waited for us to give him access to the house. Meanwhile, the overzealous guard took through the kitchen area, which was completely empty. Again, reminding us not to touch anything. Next, we walked past a large family room, a sitting area, a library, and finally, a dining room area. I looked up at the balcony in the Fourier on the second floor to see none other than Yinnsely looking down at us with her furry breed French bulldog in hand. She was shaking the dog and kissing it like it was her baby. In her other hand was her cell phone. She was screaming at someone on the other end of the phone about her children and their whereabouts. I took a quick look at Carmelo, and he looked right back at me with a devilish grin. He whispered so only I could hear him. "I know where your fucking kids are, you bitch". I made a quiet laugh and hurried behind the guard to catch up to him. Yinnsely looked stressed out. She was pacing back and forth on her balcony. I loved the feeling of seeing this woman in pain. I thought to myself. An eye for an eye, you cunt.

The guard showed us the stairs leading to the basement, where the internet box is located. We thanked him and made our way downstairs. Hoping he wouldn't follow us. But, of course, he did. With his AR.15 in hand, he walked us over to the box. Carmelo walked over to the box and started a little conversation with the guard about yesterday's soccer game, Mexico versus Venezuela. The guard instantly got excited and started raising his hands, stating, "Mexico cheated Venezuela." That gave me the perfect opportunity to set my toolbox down. Remove the holster on top where the tools were. I reached in and pulled out a Glock 17 with an extended silencer. I took aim at the guard's head, and Carmelo smiled. Carmelo signaled the guard with a head nod so that he could turn around. He had this big smile on his face that quickly turned into oh shit look. As he looked down the barrel of my gun. I could see he wanted to reach for his gun cause his fingers were searching for it, but it was too late. I took one single shot, and his brains were all over the internet box.

We found a few small windows to the rear of the house. The window had just enough space to crawl through. So, I opened the window, hoping Andrew was watching. I wasn't sure which direction he was coming from. I was just hoping no one would see him as he tried to get through this small window. I stood up, looking out the window, and out of the corner of my eye, I saw Andrew running towards the window at full speed. I quickly backed up, and he made a baseball slide straight through the window. With gun and bulletproof vest in hand, he fell five feet to the ground and onto his back as he slid through the window. He quietly said, "Woooo". Carmelo and I just smiled, shaking our heads before we turned and walked away. We both picked up our toolboxes and reached inside. We both had a Glock 17 with an extended clip, a walkie-talkie with Bluetooth earpieces, and a military-issued armor-d plated bulletproof vest inside. We quickly strapped on the vest and earpiece. We did a quick radio check with my father and Al and his team. We were all loud and clear and ready to proceed with our mission. Al deployed two drones from his spy van, and we started calling it that. The drones were able to see all heat signatures inside the home. Letting us know where every person in the house was located. It was a blessing to have the jump on each person without ever knowing we were coming. My father's job was to clear the grounds. Anyone that's a potential threat, he would illuminate them.

We quietly made our way up the steps, and Al informed us that there were two bodies in the kitchen. We slowly and quietly made our way toward Yinnsely's massive kitchen area. Andrew took the left side, Carmelo the center approach, and I came in on the right side. This way, no one missed their target. We had to be swift and precise with each kill. None of Yinnsely's guards could get a shot off, and all three of us would be dead. As per Al, he counted twelve people in the house beside us. So, we entered the kitchen area to find two of Yinnsely's guards enjoying empanadas and alcohol. I whispered to Andrew and Carmelo on three take your shots. Simultaneously, both men's bodies dropped and hit the floor at the same time. Al gave us our next target. Six of her guards were in her movie theater watching a soccer game with the volume off, so Yinnsely didn't hear them. One of the men was keeping watch by the door in case Yinnsely made her way towards that room or area. Which wasn't going to make this easy at all, but Carmelo whispered that he got it. The guard wasn't really focused on his jump at all. The game had everyone focused on the screen. Carmelo sneaked up behind the guard standing in the doorway. I snatched him up from behind by covering his mouth so he could scream or yell for help. He quickly pulled him away from the view of anyone in the room looking towards the doorway. He tried to struggle and fight, but while Carmelo was holding him firmly, I walked up and plunged my knife into his kidney and twisted the knife. Secondly, his eyes rolled over into his head and his body became lifeless. Carmelo just dropped his bloody body on the floor. Andrew whispered, "Listen, we each get two shots each, so make them count." We slowly entered the room one at a time while everyone's back was turned. Rapid fire while they sat there, knowing it was their last seconds on this earth.

We informed Al and his team that all six of the men were down, and my father informed us that three men just entered the rear of the house. We had to think fast so we didn't blow our cover or they didn't see the bodies in the kitchen. I told Carmelo and Andrew to cover me. I made my way through the kitchen quickly, right before two of the guards walked into the kitchen. I had to drop my vest and earpiece and hide my gun behind my back. I greeted the two men and was kind of baffled by the whereabouts of the third guard. One of the guards angrily told me to go fix the cable and get out of his damn way. So, I did just that and allowed him to pass me. The other guard followed behind him. The moment the first guard stepped foot into the kitchen, he noticed blood and a foot behind the island area. He attempted to hurry towards the scene but didn't notice Andrew hiding behind the wall as he walked into the kitchen. I couldn't see Andrew, but I heard the faint sound of the silencer and the guard's head exploding. Then, I instantaneously shot the second guard before he could react. The guard I shot fell on the guard Andrew shot within a microsecond, which made both of us laugh for some strange reason. Carmelo was quick to tell Al where the third guard who came in with them was. Al quickly replied he was on the toilet. Andrew and I didn't want any part of seeing a grown man shitting on the toilet. Carmelo, on the other hand, made a great point as he walked by both of us in anger. He said, "They murdered my cousin coming out the shower, so fuck it." Carmelo kicked open the bathroom door, and you could hear the man saying, "No, No, please," in Spanish. He was gone after that. Carmelo put three holes in him while he was shitting, just heartless!

At that moment, Al alerted us that a guard outside noticed one of the drones hovering above. He alerted everyone, including everyone remaining inside the mansion. He was screaming at the top of his lungs over his walk-in talkie. I grabbed my bulletproof vest and put it on quickly. We safely made our way through the house. Andrew looked at the balcony and raised his gun before I saw what he was looking at. The next we heard was a rain of gunfire coming outside, and Andrew started shooting toward the balcony with his AR.15 with a suppressor on it. But then someone from the balcony returned fire. We all took cover but Andrew. Andrew took point and gave us the chance to take cover, causing him to take two bullets to the chest. The bullets knocked him on his ass, and Carmelo took aim toward the balcony and opened fire. Andrew hit the floor pretty hard but quickly recovered and returned fire towards the balcony. I took that opportunity to retract our steps because I remember seeing another set of stairs leading to the second floor. I had to be fast cause the rain of gunfire outside could stop at any second. If that happened, they would hear their counterpart shooting at us. If Al hadn't jammed their radio and phone transmission, we would be dead for sure.

I got to the second floor and cut through two hallways to find the guard with his back against the wall. He was trying to reload and focus on what was going on below him. I just walked up behind them softly and rocked him to sleep. Two large holes in his head. I told Andrew and Carmelo to hurry up and come upstairs. They wasted no time. I could see Andrew was in pain from getting shot, so I told him to hold up here and keep an eye out. Carmelo and I searched quickly for Yinnsely, and we noticed the gunfire had stopped. What we heard next was sirens getting closer and closer. We had to hurry now. It wasn't long before she found Yinnsely in her master bathroom. She decided to hide in her tub with her dog, a 380 automatic handgun. When Carmelo walked into her bathroom, Yinnsely caught him by surprise. Yinnsely was quick to squeeze the trigger with all confidence at Carmelo's head. From my view, it looks as if the gun was jammed. She squeezed the trigger again and again. Carmelo blacked out, snatched the gun out of her hand, and punched her right in the jaw. She completely blacked out before her body hit the tub. I quickly told my father over our radio that we had her, and we needed that extraction back to the van. We tied up her hands and feet quickly and threw her over Carmelo's shoulder.

My father got the ok like it was Christmas morning, and he was ever so ready to unwrap his Christmas gifts. With his fifty-caliber short-nose sniper rifle, he was letting bodies drop one after the other. Every shot he made was a headshot. The heads of these men were looking like a destroyed watermelon beaten with a baseball bat. Andrew, Carmelo, and I made it out the front door towards the van. Andrew and I were on full alert, covering Carmelo as he brutally tossed Yinnsely headfirst into the van. We noticed three bodies on the grass and one by the front steps of the house. We could hear the siren right on top of us. We heard Al's voice over the radio instructing us to follow the road on the side of the house. It will lead us through the back entrance of the home and a small wine villa area. The road led a mile and a half before we exited onto a main road. I wanted to wait for my father to join us, but he instructed us to leave him. Al and his team packed up and left the sense the moment we told him we had the package. A mile into the drive and doing the van's top speed of 144 kilometers. We heard a huge explosion behind us. We were all looking into whatever mirrors we could find to see the explosion. It was Yinnsely's mansion up in flames. I started instantly worrying about my father, and with that thought, we noticed a brand-new Bentley convertible racing behind us. Andrew and I grabbed our rifles, ready to blow holes into this Bentley when we realized it was my father. He raced past us with a serious look on his face, and we followed him.

Chapter Fourteen
Friend or foe

We wasted no time when we got back to the hotels. Everyone was instructed to quickly pack up just what we needed within the next hour. Andrew was going to pack up Carmelo's items cause he remained in the van with Yinnsely. My father stopped a few miles from our hotel, handed a random woman in the street the keys to Bentley and walked away. He jumped in the van with us, and we dropped him off at his hotel. Once we were ready, we went back to pick him up. Paul was dressed like he had an important business meeting to attend when we pulled into the valet of his hotel. He had on dark sunglasses, a navy-blue Louis Vuitton suit, and black Louis Vuitton dress shoes. We were all confused about why he was dressed like that. We all had on sweats or cargo pants with sneakers. I moved out of the passenger seat and jumped into the back with Andrew. The moment the passenger closed, Carmelo asked, "Uncle, why are you dressed up?" My father answered, "I gave all my clothes to the hotel to dry clean and completely forgot to pick them back up. The suite was all I had, guys."
There was a short pause, and then we all busted out laughing at him.

Jaxon: Dad, are you serious?

Paul: Boy, mind your damn business. I had other things on my mind, right, Yinnsely?

Yinnsely just looked at my father with tears in her eyes. She was afraid, and we loved it. We all wanted her to suffer in the worst way. We just had no idea what my father had in store for her. We got to the airfield at 9:15 am, but our plane wasn't ready, so we had to wait an hour or so before we could take off. We requested that no flight attendants, just our pilots and copilot, be on board for the flight. The plane had to be inside a hanger so no one could see us escorting Yinnsely tied up and like beat up onto the plane. We didn't need any extra questions or witnesses. When the plane was fully gassed up and prepped for take-off. We hustled Yinnsely onto the plane while both pilot and copilot were in the cockpit. Al had given me a little needle cocktail of Zolpidem to put her to sleep instantly during the flight. Once we got her onto the planet and sat her down. Andrew put on her seat belt and lifted her shirt to inject her with the needle, and she started to really struggle and fight back. She couldn't scream because she was still gagged. Out of nowhere, my father walked up, made a fist, and pushed Yinnsely right in the mouth. She was in a daze and bleeding from her mouth and nose. Her eyes were rolled into the back of her head, so I was able to inject her without a struggle. Within three minutes, her head dropped, and she was completely incapacitated for the whole flight.

Our next stop was an airfield in Holguin, Cuba, where Erica and my family would meet us on the yacht. During the flight, my father didn't have a single conversation with us. He sat by himself, and I watched him drink a bottle and half of whiskey during the whole flight. I kept looking over at him, worried cause the man I knew as my father was gone. This man was cold, calculated, and heartless. The overwhelming guilt of my uncles, aunts, cousins, friends, and my mother was just too much for him to bear alone. I wondered if my father was too far gone to reach his soul once this was all over. Andrew saw right through me and knew I was concerned about my dad.

Andrew: Jax, Jax, he's going to be alright, bro. Uncle Paul is the strongest man we all know. His heart is broken, but he will get through it, cousin.

Jaxon: He is all I got left now.

Carmelo: You always go us, cuz!

I just smiled, but in my heart, that wasn't enough for me. My parents were my world. I didn't have the opportunity to bury my mother. None of us got that opportunity, really. After ten hours, the pilot announced we would be touching down in three minutes. I was a bit relieved that we had no kind of incidents. Yinnsely was still fast asleep with her mouth wide open. Once we were on the runway, I saw three white Escalades pulling up next to the plane. We were all a little startled and curious about who was inside these SUVs. We had no gun or any form of weapons to protect ourselves if these unknown people started shooting. I heard Andrew saying get away from the windows. So, we did just that. Then I heard my father's voice saying, "It's Erica's people, you pussies." Still, we cautiously looked out the windows as the car doors opened, and it was Bianca with her bodyguards. All heavily armed to the teeth. Carmelo was so excited to see Bianca that he ran to the door and opened it himself. Bianca's men came on board, took Yinnsely off the plane, and put her in one of the SUVs. We unloaded our personal items, and Bianca gave the pilot and copilot an extra fifty grand to keep their mouth shut on what they saw here today. The pilots took the money with extreme excitement.

From the short twenty-minute ride from the airfield, we hustled onto three small boats that shuttled us to the yacht. I was extremely excited to see my little sister and Erica. I've been daydreaming about holding her the whole flight here to Cuba. As we made our way to the top deck of the yacht, we were greeted by the entire staff, including my sister and Erica. Everyone was holding up glasses of champagne. Erica gave a short speech referring to us as gods and warriors coming home from battle. We protect the weak and strengthen family lines, our friends, and all our loved ones. Everyone cheered and drank up. Erica walked over to me and gave me the biggest hug and kiss. Her lips were so soft and vibrant. Her hold on me was everlasting. She looked me in the eye and asked me how I felt. I honestly didn't know, but she answered for me. "Jaxon, we are free, baby, we are free." I just smiled and looked around for my father and saw my sister running over to me. I gave her the biggest hug and kiss. I was glad she was safe and happy. Then, out of nowhere, Ana hugged me, stating, "My boys are safe and back to us." Well, everyone was celebrating; I just wanted to steal Erica away from everyone and bring her to my room just didn't have the balls to say.

Erica: Baby, I did all this for you. I am so proud of you.

Jaxon: Really?

Erica: Yes, you're my king!

Jaxon: Wow, king, really?

Erica: Yes, my king, and as my king, I'm going to take you up to my room, and I'm to fuck the shit out of you.

I was sipping my champagne as she whispered those words into my ear. I was so shocked by her statement I choked and had champagne running out of my nose. I had to ask her to repeat herself because I had to ensure I heard her correctly. She laughed and whispered in my ear. "Jaxon, I'm going to fuck the shit out of you." She grabbed my hand and led the way. I looked around one last time, hoping to spot my dad, who was at least enjoying himself. He wasn't, of course. He was downstairs in the ship's kitchen. Where he was holding Yinnsely and her kids naked in the deep freezer. Paul had them hanging in midair from the hands. Pouring hot water on them every thirty minutes caused their entire body to go through frostbite. He let Yinnsely kids watch as he beat her with his fist while wearing brass knuckles. Every thirty minutes till she was almost lifeless. While we partied, drank, ate, and had sex, my father was putting in work. Yinnsely died twice that night, and he had the ship's doctor on standby to revive her. Then, he would beat her back to the point of death. Andrew was curious and went down there around four am to see my father covered in Yinnsely's blood. Her kids weren't even able to cry anymore or beg for their mother's life. They were in and out of consciousness, from freezing to death. Andrew almost vomited from what he saw.

Meanwhile, I was on my back in Erica's amazing room. She had her bed covered completely in rose peddles. The lights in her room were deep red. She really set the mood with candles burning throughout the room. She had 90's R&B love songs like "Let Me Lick You Up and Down Till You Say Stop." "Let me play with your body, baby." I had one hand on Erica's hip, firmly, and the other hand on her breast as she was riding me slow and hard. She wanted to feel me deep inside her. I squeezed her fat Latin ass and big breast. She turned around and faced my feet, reverse cowgirl action, and continued to ride me. Every so often, looking back at me to see if I was in ecstasy. She reached out for my right hand and slowly sucked on my thumb, making it extremely wet. Then she directed my thumb into her anus and told me to fuck her ass with my thumb. She told me she was getting it ready cause that's where I would be putting it next. Hearing those words made my penis even harder. I refused to cum so many times. I was just holding out for her, and we did almost every position possible or could imagine. After two glorious nuts inside her, I passed out only moments later.

While in the best deep sleep of my life, I heard Erica's voice gently waking me up. Softly, her voice reached me in sleep, "Jaxon, Jaxon, I need you to wake up." I opened my eyes to find not only Erica but Bianca as well standing over me. I jumped up to grab the cover cause my balls and penis were fully uncovered. To my surprise, my hands were restricted. I pulled and yanked before I noticed that both of my hands were handcuffed to the bed. Another surprise was I was no longer in Erica's bedroom. My feet were also handcuffed. I asked them what the hell was going on. At that moment, Erica's bodyguard walked into the room and turned on all the lights, but my eyes had to adjust to the brightness. I was in the yacht theater and confused why I was there. More importantly, why did Erica and Bianca have me handcuffed to this bed? The bed was a reclining bed, so they had me sitting up in the bed and facing the theater screen.

Erica: Jaxon, while you have been asleep for the past ten hours, A lot of things had taken place while you rested your pretty little head.

Jaxon: Erica, what the fuck? What the fuck is going on? This shit ain't funny, Erica. Open these damn cuffs.

Bianca: Open; no, that won't be happening, baby. Well, Jaxon, we kinda drugged you to keep you out of the picture for a few hours while we cleaned the house.

Jaxon: Clean house, what the fuck are you two talking about? Clean house!

Erica: It's all here in this HD movie we made for you to watch. In a moment, we'll leave you alone to watch the little movie we put together for you.

As they walked out of the room, the light went out, and the screen lit up. The first thing I saw was my father in the freezer beating Yinnsely bloody half-dead body with two brace knuckles. Then, out of nowhere where the video showed someone walking up behind him. The person was built as a woman. She had polished nails, just like Bianca. They slowed down the movie so I could watch her cut my father's throat from ear to ear. I screamed at the top of my lungs, "NOOOOOOOO." The tears started pouring from my eyes. My chest felt like it was about to explode cause my heart was racing so fast. My skin felt like it was on fire. All kinds of mixed emotions were running through me. The next sense was Andrew and Carmelo gagged and handcuffed to the floorboard on the rear deck of the ship. Both were facing each other and fully naked and wet. Two men were hosing them down with high-pressure water. A voice I could not recognize on the video asked the two of them who first. Then the unrecognized voice sang Eeny, meeny, miny moe and then pointed at Andrew with his machete. He slowly walked over to Andrew and lifted the machete to his chin. He then walked behind Andrew, pulling the machete around his whole neck. He raised the machete, pointed it at the camera, and smiled. He then swung the machete like a baseball bat at Andrew's head, and I started crying even more. It took this animal three tries before he fully chopped off Andrew's head. He heartless decapitated my cousin's head from his body.

Then I heard a group of other voices in the video laughing at Carmelo because he pissed on himself. He pissed on himself from watching a man brutally chop Andrew's head off right in front of him. Carmelo had Andrew's blood running down his face and body. I begged them to stop as if they could hear me in the video. I screamed at the top of my lungs for them to stop. In case Erica and Bianca hear me outside the theater. In my head, this couldn't be real.
This had to be some sick kind of prank they were playing on me. The man picked up Andrew's head and kicked against the wall extremely hard. Andrew's blood exploded against the wall. Then, a group of men, all with knives, started stabbing Carmelo in every part of his body. His neck, his back, his chest, his head, and just continued to stabilize him. Even after he was dead. I watched his eyes closed two minutes prior, and they refused to stop stabbing his lifeless body. For two to three minutes, they just let me watch the blood pouring out of Andrew and Carmelo's bodies. Andrew's head was still rolling around. The lights in the theater came back on, and Bianca and her security guard walked back into the room. Bianca was wearing the most devilish grin on her face. She then stated, "So, Jaxon, did you like the show." I replied by telling her I'm going to kill every one of you. She smiled again and said, "Oh really." She proceeded to tell me a story.

Bianca: Did you know my mother was a nurse in the army? Who fell in love with a man while she was stationed overseas. My mother got pregnant with me, and my father never knew about it. He went back to the USA and deserted my mother and me. Years later, my mother found him in Miami. In a nightclub, she found out he was one of the owners. That night when she told him he had a daughter, he murdered my mother in front of that very nightclub. The coward didn't want my mother and me to mess up his perfect little life.

Jaxon: What the fuck is really wrong with you? Bianca, I know this story, I know this story, and you got it twisted, Bianca. My father told me every detail about your mother and how much he loved her. He never knew you even existed. Your mother died in Bahia's arms because of a drive-by shooting. A bullet that was meant for him. Something he has regretted since that day.

Erica: Shut your lying tongue. Your family has destroyed her life and countless other lives. Countless families were destroyed because of your greed and lust for power.

Jaxon: Our families are all the same. You delusional bitch. You're the daughter of a cartel boss.

Erica: Shut him the fuck up.

Jaxon: She is manipulating you, Bianca. This doesn't make any sense.

Before I could say another word, their security happily took pleasure in punching me in the Face, not once or twice, but three times. He hit so hard that I felt one of my teeth crack. I almost blacked out completely. I was hit so hard. Erica laughed as she walked out and instructed them to play the rest of the video as they all left the room. The lights went out again, and moments later, the video started. They laughingly dumped Yinnsely and her kids' bodies overboard first. Then, they dumped my father's body, followed by my cousins' bodies. The video paused for a few moments. I tried to cry and scream but couldn't find my voice, much less my breath. The weight of this pain was just too much. I was out of tears, and I just wanted to die right at that moment. I felt like a failure, a pathetic loser, and used by someone I thought loved me. The video started again, and I knew it was going to be my sister and Ana next. The video started with twelve men wearing masks and fully naked and holding their penises in their hands. They each walked into a room one by one, where Erica was waiting inside. She had her legs crossed, sitting in a large blue chair. Erica was well dressed in a blue Dior print top and bottom. She told the men no mercy and to please enjoy themselves. The video then turned to Ana. Tied up naked and gagged on a wing. Then men in masks all cheered as they took turns raping my cousin. One after another till she was bleeding from her vagina and anus. The video lasted at least an hour or so. All I could do was close my eyes, refusing to watch as these men destroyed my cousins. I could still hear every little detail taking place before the video ended. I waited in the room, but no one came to gloat over what they had done. I was just there for the next few hours with my thoughts. I wondered why Erica was doing this to me and why she just murdered my whole family. Then I wondered where Jaylyn was. What have they done to her? How was I going to get out of this alive? It seemed like hours had gone by before three men grabbed me and escorted me out of that room. Still naked and weak as they manhandled me up to the stern of the yacht. They held me up as Erica walked around me with a smile, talking and gloating about how she beat us. How she used us all to give her full control. How soon will she obtain the entire cocaine supply chain out of Colombia before the year is over?

Then Bianca made her present known a few moments later. I had my head down, feeling like a worthless failure. To hear Bianca tell Erica it's been confirmed that the captain who was loyal to my father and family. He managed to take out three of their men and flee the ship with Jaylyn. Hearing those words somehow gave me the energy and strength to fight off the two guards that were holding me up. I grabbed the guard to my right by his hair and pulled him back, kicking away his feet. He hit the ground hard and lost focus. Then, I focused all my strength on the guard to my left. I punched him twice in the face and then right into his throat. The guard grabbed his neck from the pain, and I grabbed his head and forced his entire body down toward my knee. I held his head firmly in place as I kneed him three times in the face. Then I heard a single gunshot, and I immediately felt a sharp, unbearable pain in my right waistline area. I slowly reached down to my hip before I even looked and found blood running down my leg. I turned around to see who could have shot me. Of all the people standing at a small distance, it was Erica pointing a gun at me. I took a few steps back from her and her people, and as she walked towards me. She squeezed off another round from her pistol. Hitting me in my left shoulder. I felt my life being taken from me, and I was knocked down to a knee from the blast. I slowly reached for the balcony railing to pull myself up. I got up fully, but my back was toward the balcony, and Erica shot me again, which forced me to lose my balance. I tried reaching for the balcony, but I was falling backward. Before I knew it, I was falling to my death.

I felt my body hitting the cold, dark waters incredibly hard. The enormous propeller from the yacht sucked me down into the water a few times, causing me to black out from the force. I opened my eyes a few times as I took in water in my lungs. The last time I left my body being pulled under, I hit my head and completely blacked out. I had no strength, no energy to fight for my life at this point. I knew it was my time to go. I was in the open ocean, hundreds of miles from land. Erica and her people knew that if they didn't die from the fall and gunshot wounds. Sharks would get me, and if they didn't, I would never make it shore.

In the coming months, Erica assumed control of the business that her father had intended to pass down to her. Erica had full control of eighty percent of all the cocaine that was leaving Colombia by brutal force. She spent millions on taking out smaller suppliers that didn't want to join under her umbrella. She was moving fast, swift, cunning, and heartless. Erica had bodies dropping by outrageous rates in Colombia, East London, England, California, Thailand, Bangkok, New York, Miami, Vegas, Texas, and the list goes on. She physically took her power from those who never saw her coming. As for me, I was pronounced dead with the rest of my family. My sister went into hiding in the Philippines. She worked as a hostess at the restaurant to make ends meet. Eight months to the day I was shot and left to drown when I woke up from a coma. No one knew who I was, and no one cared. I was in the care of a hospital in Kingston, Jamaica. The doctors said I had suffered tremendous memory loss from a blow to the head. All I could tell myself from looking at my body filled with holes and scars was that someone was going to pay for putting me in here.

It was only going to be a while before my memory would return, and I would know who I was and what my purpose in this life is.

Made in the USA
Columbia, SC
15 June 2024